PENGUIN BO

VIVA ZAPA

Born in Salinas, California, in 1902, JOHN STEINBECK grew up in a fertile agricultural valley about twenty-five miles from the Pacific Coast—and both valley and coast would serve as settings for some of his best fiction. In 1919 he went to Stanford University, where he intermittently enrolled in literature and writing courses until he left in 1925 without taking a degree. During the next five years he supported himself as a laborer and journalist in New York City and then as a caretaker for a Lake Tahoe estate, all the time working on his first novel, *Cup of Gold* (1929). After marriage and a move to Pacific Grove, he published two California fictions, *The Pastures of Heaven* (1932) and *To a God Unknown* (1933), and worked on short stories later collected in *The Long Valley* (1938). Popular success and financial security came only with *Tortilla Flat* (1935), stories about Monterey's paisanos. A ceaseless experimenter throughout his career, Steinbeck changed courses regularly. Three powerful novels of the late 1930s focused on the California laboring class: *In Dubious Battle* (1936), *Of Mice and Men* (1937), and the book considered by many his finest, *The Grapes of Wrath* (1939). Early in the 1940s, Steinbeck became a filmmaker with *The Forgotten Village* (1941) and a serious student of marine biology with *Sea of Cortez*. He devoted his services to the war, writing *Bombs Away* (1942) and the controversial play-novelette *The Moon Is Down* (1942). *Cannery Row* (1945), *The Wayward Bus* (1947), *The Pearl* (1947), *A Russian Journal* (1948), another experimental drama, *Burning Bright* (1950), and *The Log from the* Sea of Cortez (1951) preceded publication of the monumental *East of Eden* (1952), an ambitious saga of the Salinas Valley and his own family's history. The last decades of his life were spent in New York City and Sag Harbor with his third wife, with whom he traveled widely. Later books include *Sweet Thursday* (1954), *The Short Reign of Pippin IV: A Fabrication* (1957), *Once There Was a War* (1958), *The Winter of Our Discontent* (1961), *Travels with Charley in Search of America* (1962), *America and Americans* (1966), and the posthumously published *Journal of a Novel: The* East of Eden *Letters* (1969), *Viva Zapata!* (1975), *The Acts of King Arthur and His Noble Knights* (1976), and *Working Days: The Journals of* The Grapes of Wrath (1989). He died in 1968, having won a Nobel Prize in 1962.

BY JOHN STEINBECK

FICTION

Cup of Gold
The Pastures of Heaven
To a God Unknown
Tortilla Flat
In Dubious Battle
Saint Katy the Virgin
Of Mice and Men
The Red Pony
The Long Valley
The Grapes of Wrath

The Moon Is Down
Cannery Row
The Wayward Bus
The Pearl
Burning Bright
East of Eden
Sweet Thursday
The Winter of Our Discontent
The Short Reign of Pippin IV

Las uvas de la ira *(Spanish-language edition of* The Grapes of Wrath*)*
The Acts of King Arthur and His Noble Knights

NONFICTION

Sea of Cortez: A Leisurely Journal of Travel and Research
(in collaboration with Edward F. Ricketts)
Bombs Away: The Story of a Bomber Team
A Russian Journal *(with pictures by Robert Capa)*
The Log from the *Sea of Cortez*
Once There Was a War
Travels with Charley in Search of America
America and Americans
Journal of a Novel: The *East of Eden* Letters
Working Days: The Journals of *The Grapes of Wrath*

PLAYS

Of Mice and Men
The Moon Is Down

COLLECTIONS

The Portable Steinbeck
The Short Novels of John Steinbeck
Steinbeck: A Life in Letters

OTHER WORKS

The Forgotten Village *(documentary)*
Zapata *(includes the screenplay* of Viva Zapata!*)*

CRITICAL LIBRARY EDITION

The Grapes of Wrath *(edited by Peter Lisca)*

Emiliano Zapata

The Original Screenplay by JOHN STEINBECK

Edited by Robert E. Morsberger

Penguin Books

PENGUIN BOOKS

Published by the Penguin Group
Penguin Group (USA) Inc., 375 Hudson Street, New York, New York 10014, U.S.A.
Penguin Group (Canada), 90 Eglinton Avenue East, Suite 700, Toronto,
Ontario, Canada M4P 2Y3 (a division of Pearson Penguin Canada Inc.)
Penguin Books Ltd, 80 Strand, London WC2R 0RL, England
Penguin Ireland, 25 St Stephen's Green, Dublin 2, Ireland (a division of Penguin Books Ltd)
Penguin Group (Australia), 250 Camberwell Road, Camberwell
Victoria 3124, Australia (a division of Pearson Australia Group Pty Ltd)
Penguin Books India Pvt Ltd, 11 Community Centre, Panchsheel Park, New Delhi – 110 017, India
Penguin Group (NZ), 67 Apollo Drive, Rosedale, North Shore 0632,
New Zealand (a division of Pearson New Zealand Ltd)
Penguin Books (South Africa) (Pty) Ltd, 24 Sturdee Avenue,
Rosebank, Johannesburg 2196, South Africa

Penguin Books Ltd, Registered Offices:
80 Strand, London WC2R 0RL, England

First published in the United States of America by The Viking Press, Inc. 1975
Published in Penguin Books 2009

Copyright © Elaine Steinbeck, 1975
Copyright © Penguin Group (USA) Inc., 1965
All rights reserved

Page viii constitutes an extension of this copyright page.
All photographs courtesy of Twentieth Century-Fox Film Corporation

LIBRARY OF CONGRESS CATALOGING IN PUBLICATION DATA
Steinbeck, John, 1902–1968.
Viva Zapata! The original screenplay.
Bibliography: p.
1. Zapata, Emiliano, 1979–1919—Drama.
[1. Viva Zapata! [Motion Picture]]
PN 1997.V56 1975 812'.5'2 74-7659
ISBN 978-0-670-00579-6

Printed in the United States of America

Steinbeck Vive!

ACKNOWLEDGMENTS

I should like to express my gratitude to Elaine Steinbeck, Elia Kazan, John Womack, Jr., Herbert Kline, and Richard Astro for generously providing correspondence and taking the time to answer questions about John Steinbeck and *Viva Zapata!* Katherine Lambert, Frances C. Richardson, and Kenneth Kenyon of the Research Department at Twentieth Century-Fox made the resources of the studio files available. A slightly different version of "Steinbeck's Zapata: Rebel versus Revolutionary" was published in 1971 by the Oregon State University Press in *Steinbeck: The Man and His Work*, edited by Richard Astro and Tetsumaro Hayashi, Copyright © 1971 by Richard Astro and Tetsumaro Hayashi; the essay is reprinted here, with slight modifications, by permission of the Oregon State University Press. "Steinbeck's Screenplays and Productions" originally appeared in a slightly different form in *A Study Guide to Steinbeck*, edited by Tetsumaro Hayashi, Copyright © 1974 by Tetsumaro Hayashi, published by The Scarecrow Press, Inc. I also wish to thank Denis Halliwell of The Viking Press for editorial assistance. Thanks are inadequate for the suggestions and moral support provided by my wife in all stages of this project, from its inception to the final proofreading.

CONTENTS

Steinbeck's Zapata: Rebel versus Revolutionary   xi

Credits   xxxiii

A Note on the Script   xxxv

Viva Zapata!   1

Steinbeck's Screenplays and Productions   123

Steinbeck's Films   145

Bibliography   149

STEINBECK'S ZAPATA:

REBEL VERSUS REVOLUTIONARY

In his studies of rebellion, Albert Camus makes an essential distinction between the rebel and the revolutionary. The rebel is an independent nonconformist protesting regimentation and oppression. He stands for freedom, and he is willing to die for it but reluctant to kill for it. If he backs the appeal to arms, he stops short of tyranny. The revolutionary, by contrast, speaks of liberty but establishes terror; in the name of equality and fraternity, he sets up the guillotine or the firing squad. For the sake of an abstract mankind, he finds it expedient to purge the unorthodox individual, to institutionalize terror, to enshrine dogma and dialectic. The rebel is like Socrates, Thoreau, or Martin Luther King, whereas the revolutionary is Saint-Just, Robespierre, Lenin, Stalin, and the enslaving liberators of the twentieth century. Camus states that "the great event of the twentieth century was the forsaking of the values of freedom by the revolutionary movement," which contended "that we needed justice first and that we could come to freedom later on, as if slaves could ever hope to achieve justice."[1] On the other hand, "The rebel undoubtedly demands a certain degree of freedom for himself; but in no case, if he is consistent, does he demand the right to destroy the existence and the freedom of others. He humiliates no one. . . . He is not only the slave against the master, but also man against the world of master and slave."[2]

This distinction runs throughout the work of John

[1] Albert Camus, *Resistance, Rebellion, and Death*, trans. Justin O'Brien (New York: Alfred A. Knopf, 1961), pp. 90–91.
[2] Camus, *The Rebel*, trans. Anthony Bower (New York: Alfred A. Knopf, Vintage Books, 1957), p. 284.

Steinbeck and receives its most explicit treatment in his screenplay *Viva Zapata!*, which Elia Kazan made into one of the more successful movies of 1952. Unlike Steinbeck's earlier scripts for *Lifeboat* and *A Medal for Benny*, this was not a collaboration; Steinbeck alone wrote both the story and the script. He worked on *Zapata* from the fall of 1948 until May 1950, and then went on location during the filming. The finished film was very much Steinbeck's statement. It puts into final focus issues with which he had been concerned for the previous twenty years and clarifies the relationship of issues to individuals and leaders to people. The conflict between creative dissent and intolerant militancy has a timeless relevancy, and *Zapata* deserves a close analysis both as a social statement and a work of art.

As a study of leadership and insurrection, *Zapata* has roots in *In Dubious Battle*, *The Grapes of Wrath*, and *The Moon Is Down*. The protagonists of *In Dubious Battle* are Communists; but despite its sympathy for the strikers, the novel is profoundly critical of revolutionist tactics. Steinbeck commented that "Communists will hate it and the other side will too."[3] The battle is indeed dubious, for the means do not justify the end. Mac, the Communist organizer, is the professional and ruthless revolutionary to whom people are merely tools of guerrilla warfare. Zapata is given leadership by the already aroused people, but Mac is the manipulator who instigates a strike that he knows will fail and that is part of "the long view" toward a brave new world. For the cause, it does not matter which individuals suffer. To win the workers' confidence, Mac risks the life of a woman in labor. He exploits the death of friends, for "We've got to use what-

---

[3] Peter Lisca, "John Steinbeck: A Literary Biography," *Steinbeck and His Critics*, E. W. Tedlock, Jr., and C. V. Wicker, eds. (Albuquerque: University of New Mexico Press, 1957), p. 10.

ever material comes to us."[4] He hopes some of the strikers will be killed, for "If they knock off some of the tramps we have a public funeral; and after that, we get some real action"; and when he is told that innocent men may be shot, he replies, "In a war a general knows he's going to lose men."[5] Mac advises Jim Nolan, the Communist novice, "Don't you go liking people, Jim. We can't waste time liking people."[6]

Thus for the determined revolutionary, issues are more important than individuals. Jim Nolan is human enough at first, but he develops into such a True Believer that his "cold thought to fight madness" scares even Mac. When Mac smashes the face of a high-school boy, Jim says, "he's not a kid, he's an example . . . a danger to the cause," and beating him "was an operation, that's all."[7] Mac now feels that Jim is not human, but Jim insists that "Sympathy is as bad as fear."[8] Like Ethan Brand, he has lost his hold on humanity and justifies torture in the name of human brotherhood.

Mac and Jim rarely discuss dialectic; they seem motivated less by party dogma than by a need for the transfiguring experience of revolution that Doc Burton calls "Pure religious ecstasy."[9] The two Communists awaiting martyrdom in "Raid" have a similar emotion; but as Camus notes, "Politics is not religion, or if it is, then it is nothing but the Inquisition."[10]

In reaction to *In Dubious Battle* and *The Grapes of Wrath*, some right-wing critics of the time denounced

[4] John Steinbeck, *In Dubious Battle* (New York: Viking Compass Books, 1963), p. 53.
[5] *Ibid.*, p. 305.
[6] *Ibid.*, p. 103.
[7] *Ibid.*, pp. 247–49.
[8] *Ibid.*, p. 249.
[9] *Ibid.*, p. 231.
[10] Camus, *The Rebel*, p. 302.

Steinbeck as a revolutionary, even as a Communist. It is no longer necessary to refute these charges; Steinbeck was never a Communist except in Mr. Hines's sense that "A red is any son-of-a-bitch that wants thirty cents an hour when we're payin' twenty-five!"[11] In Russia, critics noted that *The Grapes of Wrath* did not follow the ortho- dox party line, but B. Balasov said the book has a "defi- nite revolutionary direction."[12] Actually, as Chester E. Eisinger and others have pointed out, Steinbeck's migra- tory farm workers have their roots in Jeffersonian agrar- ianism. Far from wanting state collectivism, they long, like Lennie and George in *Of Mice and Men*, for a place of their own. Steinbeck was an ardent advocate of private property and wrote in *The Grapes of Wrath*, "If a man owns a little property, that property is him . . . and some way he's bigger because he owns it."[13]

Steinbeck predicted that if revolution should come, it would not be the work of professional agitators but would be an overflow of outrage in response to organized oppression. Under conditions of farm labor in California, "the dignity of the man is attacked. No trust is accorded them. They are surrounded as though it were suspected that they would break into revolt at any moment. It would seem that a surer method of forcing them to revolt could not be devised."[14] Steinbeck's solution was punishment of vigilante terrorism and encouragement for the agricul- tural workers to organize within a democratic frame- work.[15] Camus notes that "a change of regulations concerning property without a corresponding change of

[11] Steinbeck, *The Grapes of Wrath* (New York: The Viking Press, 1939), p. 407.

[12] James W. Tuttleton, "Steinbeck in Russia: The Rhetoric of Praise and Blame," *Modern Fiction Studies*, 11 (Spring 1965), 80.

[13] Steinbeck, *The Grapes of Wrath*, p. 50.

[14] Steinbeck, *Their Blood Is Strong* (San Francisco: Simon J. Lubin Society of California, Inc., 1938), p. 13.

[15] *Ibid.*, p. 29.

government is not a revolution but a reform,"[16] and this is what Steinbeck supported. But unless it came quickly, he predicted that "from pain, hunger, and despair the whole mass of labor will revolt."[17]

Such a spontaneous uprising of the people occurs in *Viva Zapata!* Emiliano Zapata is not a conscious revolutionary but a natural leader of a justifiably rebellious peasantry. In the film, he first appears as a member of a delegation to the dictator Díaz. Like the dispossessed Okies of *The Grapes of Wrath*, the farmers complain that an anonymous "they" have taken the village land. The delegates claim ownership since before history—reinforced by papers from the Spanish crown and the Mexican Republic. The question of ownership is recurrent and critical to Steinbeck. In *The Grapes of Wrath* and *Their Blood Is Strong*, he urges not collectivism but a fair redistribution of land among private holders. Later in *Viva Zapata!*, when Don Nacio, a landowner sympathetic to the peasants, entertains some large planters, he defends the Indian villagers' right to their land and urges the planters to "Give the land back. You don't need it. You have so much. . . . We're all in danger. If we don't give a little—we'll lose it all."[18] Don García replies indignantly that he paid for the land and therefore owns it, but Don Nacio insists that the Indians lived there for a thousand years, "since before the Conquest," and that such living makes them the true owners. His attitude, and that of the peasants, is like the tenant men in *The Grapes of Wrath* who say, ". . . it's our land. We measured it and broke it up. We were born on it, and we got killed on it, died on it. Even if it's no good, it's still ours. That's what makes it ours—being born on it, working it, dying

[16] Camus, *The Rebel*, p. 106.
[17] Steinbeck, *Their Blood Is Strong*, p. 30.
[18] All quotations from *Viva Zapata!* are from Steinbeck's shooting final script, May 16, 1951.

on it. That makes ownership, not a paper with numbers on it."[19]

Zapata's role is that of agrarian reformer, not a revolutionary remolder of society. When Díaz questions the delegation's ownership of the land, Zapata emerges as spokesman for the group. He speaks common sense and farmers' folkways, not dialectic, and tells Díaz that corn, not the courts, is essential to the farmers. When Díaz advises the men to check the boundaries but refuses them official permission to cross guarded fences to do so, Zapata replies that they will take his advice. We then see a close-up of Díaz's hand circling Zapata's name on the list of delegates.

Though he is more articulate than the others and takes more initiative, Zapata does not seek leadership; circumstances and the people thrust it upon him. Steinbeck shows the revolution beginning as at Concord and Lexington; the embattled farmers trying to survey their lands are attacked by Rurales, who begin machine-gunning them. Zapata, who is mounted, lassoes the machine gun and enables most of the farmers to escape. Here and in later episodes, he has no plans but rather an impetuous reaction to tyrannic violence. But as the Mayor in *The Moon Is Down* tells Alex Morden, who hit and killed a Nazi overseer, "Your private anger was the beginning of a public anger."[20] Likewise Casy and Tom Joad at first have only a spontaneous and improvised response to episodes of outrage, but gradually they learn to make long-range plans.

Zapata meanwhile hides in the hills with a handful of followers. There he is sought out by Fernando Aguirre, who first appears as a young man with a typewriter, which he calls "the sword of the mind." Zapata at this point is still illiterate; he is no intellectual but is in tune

[19] Steinbeck, *The Grapes of Wrath*, p. 45.
[20] Steinbeck, *The Moon Is Down* (New York: The Viking Press, 1942), p. 96.

with the ways of people and the land. One of the more moving scenes in the film is his urgent plea on his wedding night that his wife teach him to read. It is significant that he speaks Aztec as well as Spanish; this enables him both to get information from the peasants and to hear and empathize with their sufferings. Unlike this man of the people, Fernando has no background that we ever discover; we gradually learn that he is the revolutionary who will betray anyone for his own ends. Fernando comes as an emissary from Madero, "the leader of the fight against Díaz." Before agreeing to become an ally, Zapata sends his friend Pablo to Texas to look in Madero's face and report what he sees; Zapata wants to evaluate a man, not an ideology.

While Pablo is away, Zapata receives a pardon from the charges that resulted when he attacked the Rurales and is hired to appraise horses for his wealthy patron, Don Nacio. He begins courting the wealthy, aristocratic Josefa Espejo. Zapata now has a private life to lead and a promising future. But again, indignation intervenes. Camus notes that "rebellion does not arise only, and necessarily, among the oppressed, but . . . it can also be caused by the mere spectacle of oppression of which someone else is the victim. In such cases there is a feeling of identification with another individual."[21] Steinbeck composes such a scene very carefully. We first see eggs being beaten for rubbing down Arabian stallions. A hungry little girl dips her finger into the mixture and licks it. The mother, seeing Zapata observe this, slaps the child, who looks away in shame, and Zapata also looks away in shame. The manager says such people are lazy and orders servants to rub down the horses better. When the manager beats a starving boy whom he catches stealing food from the horses, Zapata can no longer stand by; he risks his job and his pardon by knocking the man

[21] Camus, The Rebel, p. 16.

down. Zapata's employer asks, "Are you responsible for everybody? You can't be the conscience of the whole world," but Zapata can only answer, "He was hungry." Yet Zapata does not want involvement; he longs for privacy, and so he apologizes to the manager. At this strategic moment, Pablo returns from Madero, accompanied by Fernando, who offers Zapata a command. Zapata's response is that he does not want to be a leader: "I don't want to be the conscience of the world. I don't want to be the conscience of anybody."

Yet he cannot be passive in the face of oppression. Later, when he encounters Rurales dragging a prisoner by a noose, Zapata cuts the man loose and becomes an outlaw a second time. Like a migrant from *The Grapes of Wrath*, this man (significantly named Innocente) had crawled through a fence at night to plant a little corn. Again, Zapata has no plan but improvises in reaction to events. Fernando, the revolutionary, however, has plans and he does not object to the sacrifice of the individual. Fernando smiles when Zapata rides off an outlaw. Zapata can serve the cause, and his private misfortune may be public good.

Camus observes that "when a movement of rebellion begins, suffering is seen as a collective experience"; the rebel "identifies himself with a natural community."[22] Likewise, Steinbeck notes in *Sea of Cortez*: "Non-teleological notion: that the people we call leaders are simply those who, at the given moment, are moving in the direction behind which will be found the greatest weight, and which represents a future mass movement."[23] This is what now happens to Zapata. When Rurales capture him, the people accompany him in an increasingly massive procession until it is so large that it stops the column.

[22] *Ibid.*, pp. 22, 16.
[23] Steinbeck, *Sea of Cortez: A Leisurely Journal of Travel and Research*, in collaboration with Edward F. Ricketts (New York: The Viking Press, 1941), p. 138.

The mere presence of this silent, spontaneous procession forces the captain to free the prisoner. The people bring Zapata's white horse and by this gesture make him their leader. Before, he had no followers, only a handful of friends; now he takes command. Fernando urges him to cut the telegraph wires. "Captain. 'Don't touch that! This is rebellion!' " In a fine dramatic pause, Zapata looks at his brother Eufemio, whose machete is raised; then he orders, "Cut it."

The film has been building symbolically to this moment. First, Zapata has overseen the cutting of the boundary wire. Next, he has cut the noose around Innocente's neck—but too late; the soldiers have dragged the man to his death, and Zapata concludes that he should have cut the rope first and then talked. After that, we see Zapata himself pulled by a halter. Thus, cutting the wire becomes a symbolic culmination, severing the bonds of oppression and signifying decisive action.

The film now presents a number of quick scenes of guerrilla warfare culminating in Díaz's defeat. Zapata says thankfully, "The fighting is over." This campaign has been like the first or real Russian Revolution, and fully half of the script deals with it. But instead of bringing peace and reform, the revolution is spoiled by the professionals, who inaugurate a series of betrayals. In a dramatically symbolic scene, Steinbeck shows Zapata first torn between the conflicting claims of power and the people. As the victorious Zapatistas are celebrating, Fernando arrives with a document from Madero designating Zapata "General of the Armies of the South." Brother Eufemio hands him a general's ornaments, while an Indian woman gratefully gives him "a dirty bouquet of live trussed chickens"; the last shot shows him standing with the chickens in one hand and the ornaments in the other. It is significant that Fernando is the emissary for power. Reveling in victory, the celebrants all get drunk except Fernando, who remains cold sober.

EUFEMIO: I know what's the matter with you. You are unhappy because the fighting is over.

FERNANDO (*muttering to himself*): Half victories! All this celebrating and nothing really won!

EUFEMIO (*embracing him*): I love you—but I don't like you. I've never liked you.

FERNANDO (*still going on*): There will have to be a lot more blood shed.

EUFEMIO (*losing patience with him*): All right! There *will* be! But not tonight! (*gives him bottle*) Here—enjoy yourself! Be human!

It is never clear what Fernando wants or why he thinks there must be bloodshed, but he is intolerant of anything less than absolutism. He resembles Jim Nolan when the latter declares, "I'm stronger than you, Mac. I'm stronger than anything in the world, because I'm going in a straight line. You and all the rest have to think of women and tobacco and liquor and keeping warm and fed."[24]

Madero is now in charge. He is presented as a good man, mild and well-meaning, but bewildered. When Zapata presses him for immediate land reform, Madero insists that rebuilding must take time and be done carefully under the law. Zapata is impatient, though willing to give Madero a chance, but Fernando condemns the President as an enemy.

PABLO: But you're his emissary, his officer, his friend. . . .

FERNANDO: I'm a friend to no one—and to nothing except logic. . . . This is the time for killing!

For the True Believer, the revolutionary fanatic like Fernando, there can be no redemption without the shedding of blood. Camus notes that by contrast, "Authentic acts of rebellion will only consent to take up arms for

[24] Steinbeck, *In Dubious Battle*, p. 249.

institutions that limit violence, not for those which codify it."[25]

Fernando apparently wants a purge, and with some reason, for as the delegation departs, Huerta and a group of fellow generals enter and dominate Madero. Huerta advises him to shoot Zapata now, but Madero insists that he does not shoot his own people and that Zapata is an honest man. With true totalitarian logic, Huerta replies, "What has that got to do with it??!! A man can be honest and completely wrong!" From here on, Zapata's inevitable death is foreshadowed, and the film takes a tragic turn.

While the guerrillas are disarming under Madero's orders, Huerta and the regular army pull a coup and march against Morelos. Madero has been like Kerensky, insisting on a constitutional government; now the ruthless professionals take over. Madero falls into Huerta's hands and is murdered. The Zapatistas resume their guerrilla warfare against the new oppressor. Again Zapata is victorious; but in the process, power inevitably involves him in evil. Camus asks "whether innocence, the moment it becomes involved in action, can avoid committing murder."[26] Zapata's forces are ambushed, and among the suspected traitors is Pablo, accused of meeting with Madero after Huerta betrayed the revolution. Pablo's defense is an eloquent plea for peace. Madero, he says, was trying to hold Huerta in check.

> PABLO: . . . He was a good man, Emiliano. He wanted to build houses and plant fields. And he was right. If we could begin to build—even while the burning goes on. If we could plant while we destroy . . .

Fernando interrupts harshly, "You deserted our cause!"

[25] Camus, *The Rebel*, p. 292.
[26] *Ibid.*, p. 4.

PABLO: Our cause was land—not a thought, but corn-planted earth to feed the families. And Liberty—not a word, but a man sitting safely in front of his house in the evening. And Peace—not a dream, but a time of rest and kindness. The question beats in my head, Emiliano. Can a good thing come from a bad act? Can peace come from so much killing? Can kindness finally come from so much violence? (*he now looks directly into* EMILIANO's *immobile eyes*) And can a man whose thoughts are born in anger and hatred, can such a man lead to peace? And govern in peace?

This point becomes the focus of the rest of the film, and it is an issue that concerned Steinbeck for a long time. Doc Burton, his spokesman in *In Dubious Battle*, tells Jim: "In my little experience the end is never very different in its nature from the means. Damn it, Jim, you can only build a violent thing with violence." When Jim insists, "All great things have violent beginnings," Doc replies: "We fight ourselves and we can only win by killing every man."[27]

Eventually, Fernando helps to kill Zapata; but meanwhile his inflexible logic requires the death of Pablo, even though it was Fernando who first brought Pablo and Madero together. Now he tries to make even Zapata his tool. While Zapata himself is executing Pablo at the latter's request, a courier arrives and Fernando informs him, "General Zapata is busy." We hear the shot that kills Pablo; and Fernando then says "General Zapata will see you now." Only once before had Emiliano been called "General Zapata," and that too was by Fernando. Otherwise, he had been simply a *campesino*, always approachable, as when a young boy, who like Zapata had lassoed a machine gun, demanded Zapata's white horse when offered a reward. Zapata's giving the horse to him fore-

[27] Steinbeck, *In Dubious Battle*, p. 230.

shadows his renouncing power and returning it to the people. Now, setting up formal audiences and executive isolation, Fernando has become a barrier between Zapata and the people.

When some of the people turn against him, Zapata realizes that Pablo was right. Pablo, in his patience and wisdom, resembles Anselmo in *For Whom the Bell Tolls*; his friend the Soldadera, a Pilar-type woman warrior, tries to kill Zapata with Pablo's knife. The guards urge her death, but Zapata lets her go, insisting, "The killing must stop! Pablo said it. That's all I know how to do!" Whenever he has been tempted to act the tyrant, one of the people has reminded him of reality.

Zapata's refusal to take any rewards for himself leads to his death. Huerta is beaten, and Fernando and Villa propose Zapata for President. Though he refuses office, Zapata does take command in Mexico City, while Carranza and Obregón replace Huerta as the military opposition. An Old General proposes that Zapata form an alliance with these commanders "for the good of Mexico." Intervening, Fernando violently refuses, insisting, "The principle of successful rule is always the same. There can be no opposition. Of course, our ends are different." He advises Zapata to kill the General; yet when Zapata relinquishes power, it is Fernando who joins Carranza and Obregón and gives the Old General the plan that betrays Zapata and leads to his death.

Again, it is a reminder from the people that recalls Zapata from power. A delegation from Morelos calls upon him to complain that his brother Eufemio has been taking their lands and women. Zapata at first equivocates, asks for time, then (in a re-enactment of the first audience with Díaz) circles the name of the spokesman for the group. Suddenly, with horror, he realizes what he is doing and what he is about to become. He rejoins his people, saying, "I'm going home. . . . I'm going home. There are some things I forgot."

FERNANDO: So you're throwing it away. . . . I promise you you won't live long. . . . In the name of all *we* fought for, don't leave here!

EMILIANO: In the name of all *I* fought for, I'm going. [editor's italics]

FERNANDO: Thousands of men have died to give you power and you're throwing it away.

EMILIANO: I'm taking it back where it belongs; to thousands of men.

When Fernando refuses to go with him, Zapata says, "Now I know you. No wife, no woman, no home, no field. You do not gamble, drink, no friends, no love. . . . You only destroy. . . . I guess that's your love. . . ."

In this context Zapata's love story is significant. The courtship and marriage of Zapata and Josefa (the only treatment of romantic love Steinbeck had so far written) is historically oversimplified but artistically valid. The real Zapata had dozens of women and numerous bastards. The screen Zapata is more saintly, but the love story humanizes him, adds a tragic dimension, and also enables Steinbeck to include some humor and folklore. In a picaresque episode, Zapata and Eufemio first approach Josefa and her aunt in church; the outlaw proposes while she is praying. Her father has predicted that Zapata's wife will become a peasant, and she rejects her suitor with the words: "I have no intention of ending up washing clothes in a ditch and patting tortillas like an Indian." Later, Zapata courts her more formally in a humorous scene with traditionally stilted proverbs; the tiger is momentarily tamed. The drama of their wedding night, when she starts teaching him to read while crowds celebrate outside, is moving; they are like earnest and innocent children with the book between them. Josefa does not appear again until near the end, when we see her washing in a stream with Indian women. "Her father's prediction has come true—she is practically indistinguishable from the others." But she is ennobled, not debased, by the change. Though she appears in only five comparatively brief scenes, the part is memorable, with humor, humanity, and pathos. The script conveys a sense of their whole life together, and her anguish on the eve of the fatal ambush is the climax of Zapata's sacrifice.

Once home, Zapata initiates a program of planting and building along with the fighting against Carranza and Obregón, and tells the people:

> About leaders. You've looked for leaders. For strong men without faults. There aren't any. These are only men like yourselves. . . . There's no leader but yourselves.

Thus when Fernando accomplishes Zapata's betrayal and murder, the people can go on.

In *The Moon Is Down*, the Nazi conquerors insist that Mayor Orden think for his people and keep them in order. Orden replies that his people "don't like to have others think for them" and that "authority is in the town," not in any individual.[28] Corell, the quisling traitor, tells the Nazis, "When we have killed the leaders, the rebellion will be broken."[29] This issue had long been of concern to Steinbeck. Considering Steinbeck's self-reliant reformers, Frederic I. Carpenter asked in 1941, "What if this self-reliance lead to death? What if the individual is killed before the social group is saved?"[30] Though the Nazis do order the Mayor's death, Dr. Winter observes: "They think that just because they have only one leader and one head, we are all like that . . . but we are a free people; we have as many heads as we have people, and in a time of need leaders pop up among us like mushrooms."[31]

[28] Steinbeck, *The Moon Is Down*, pp. 36, 41.
[29] *Ibid.*, p. 171.
[30] Frederic I. Carpenter, "The Philosophical Joads," *College English*, II (January 1941), 325.
[31] Steinbeck, *The Moon Is Down*, p. 175.

Zapata's wife, fearing a trap, asks, "If anything happens to you, what would become of these people? What would they have left?" His answer is, "Themselves."

> JOSEFA: With all the fighting and the death, what has changed?
> EMILIANO: *They've* changed. That is how things really change—slowly—through people. They don't need me any more.
> JOSEFA: They have to be lead.
> EMILIANO: But by each other. A strong man makes a weak people. Strong people don't need a strong man.

A passage from *The Grapes of Wrath* anticipates the ending of *Zapata*. When Tom Joad leaves to become a rebel against oppression, Ma tells him, "They might kill ya."

> Tom laughed uneasily. "Well, maybe like Casy says, a fella ain't got a soul of his own, but on'y a piece of a big one—an' then—"
> "Then what, Tom?"
> "Then it don' matter. Then I'll be aroun' in the dark. Then I'll be ever'where—wherever you look."[32]

Perhaps the people don't need a leader, but they need a legend. When Zapata is shot to ribbons from ambush, some of the peasants emerge. The Soldadera, who had tried to kill Zapata, now composes his body, for his death is an atonement that makes him again one of her people. Lazaro, an old veteran who knew Zapata well, examines the body and spurns it, saying that such a shot-up corpse could be anybody. ". . . I fought with him all these years. Do they think they can fool me? They can't kill him. . . ."

> YOUNG MAN (*agreeing*): They'll never get him. Can you capture a river? Can you kill the wind?

[32] Steinbeck, *The Grapes of Wrath*, p. 572.

LAZARO: No! He's not a river and he's not the wind! He's a man—and they still can't kill him! . . . He's in the mountains. You couldn't find him now. But if we ever need him again—he'll be back.

As they look up to the mountains, they see Zapata's white horse, which escaped and which is now walking toward the peak.

At first this may seem like a conventional Hollywood ending, but in fact it is historically and artistically appropriate. If Lazaro's name recalls Lazarus and thus links Zapata with Christ, there is a Mexican context for resurrection as well in the Montezuma myth that makes the slain emperor into a once and future king. Many of the people of Morelos did indeed refuse to believe that Zapata was dead; some insisted the corpse was not his, and others claimed to have seen his horse galloping into the southern mountains. In actuality, Zapata was not alone but accompanied by a bodyguard when he was killed, and his horse was not white but sorrel. The white horse comes from Diego Rivera's mural of Zapata. Thus slight distortions of fact may come closer to the ultimate meaning of Zapata's death.

Some movie reviewers faulted the film for simplifying or distorting history, but the simplification is a virtue here. Steinbeck cuts through the complexities of campaigns and the incredible intricacies of political intrigues to get at what he sees as the essence of the events. The latter is what most bothered some reviewers. The movie had a mixed reception, praise going to the action sequences and to performances by Anthony Quinn (who won an Academy Award) as Eufemio, Joseph Wiseman as Fernando, and Harold Gordon as Madero, with divided opinion on the effectiveness of Jean Peters as Josefa and Marlon Brando as Zapata. *Newsweek*'s reviewer called the film a "sincere tribute" with "a careful and intelligent characterization"; *The Christian Century* found it "brilliant"; *Commonweal* termed it "a thoughtful film"; and the Chief of the American History Division of the New York Public Library praised it as "exciting and impressive."[33] But *Holiday* complained of a "tedious and oratorical screenplay by John Steinbeck"; *Life* lamented Steinbeck's "mouthfuls of political platitudes"; *The New Yorker* found the film entertaining aside from "Mr. Steinbeck's murky views on revolution"; and *The New Republic* objected to "squelchy aphorisms of a kind we have had before from the Oakies [sic] of California and the doomed heroes of the Norwegian underground."[34]

Actually, resemblances to *The Grapes of Wrath* and *The Moon Is Down* reveal a continuity in Steinbeck's intellectual concerns, no more reprehensible than the reappearance of central themes in the work of Hawthorne and Henry James. A study of *Zapata* can enrich one's appreciation of the earlier books. The aphorisms occur in an appropriate context of action, and they by no means constitute the greater part of the script. The philosophizing is dramatic as well as didactic. For instance, Zapata's statements that, "There's no leader but yourselves" and that "a strong people is the only lasting strength" occur when the men of Morelos have asked him to punish his brother for stealing land and women. Zapata cannot kill his brother, but his speech (which also prophesies his own death) suggests what they must do. While he is still talking, Eufemio is killed in the hallway. Far from being sententious, Zapata's speech is tense with terror. When Hollis Alpert complained of so-called "stock phrases" like "A strong people does not need a strong man," Laura

[33] *Newsweek*, 34 (February 4, 1952), 78; *The Christian Century*, 69 (April 23, 1952), 510; Philip T. Hartung, *Commonweal*, 55 (February 29, 1952), 517; Gerold D. McDonald, *Library Journal*, 77 (February 15, 1952), 311.

[34] *Holiday*, 11 (May 1952), 105; *Life*, 32 (February 25, 1952), 61; John McCarten, "Wool from the West," *The New Yorker*, 27 (February 16, 1952), 106; *The New Republic*, 126 (February 25, 1952), 21.

Z. Hobson asked Steinbeck about them, and he replied: "I interviewed every living person I could find in Mexico who had known or fought with Zapata. Again and again I heard those words or their first cousins." Against charges of bombast and cliché, he said, "Whenever a man disagrees with the ideas involved in a book, a play, or a movie, and cannot publicly admit his disagreement, he attacks on grounds of grammar or technique."[35]

Elia Kazan has explained some of the political pressures brought against the film. Noting that the Mexican revolution had other leaders besides Zapata, he claimed that he and Steinbeck were particularly fascinated by Zapata's renunciation of power in the moment of victory. "We felt this act of renunciation was the high point of our story and the key to Zapata himself." When they submitted the script for the opinion of some prominent Mexican film-makers, these men "attacked with sarcastic fury our emphasis on his refusal to take power." Kazan claims that he and Steinbeck felt such criticism came from Mexican Communists who wanted "to capitalize on the people's reverence for Zapata by working his figure into their propaganda. . . . Nearly two years later our guess was confirmed by a rabid attack on the picture in the *Daily Worker*, which parallels everything the two Mexicans argued, and which all but implies that John invented Zapata's renunciation of power. No Communist, no totalitarian, ever refused power. By showing that Zapata did this, we spoiled a poster figure that the Communists have been at some pains to create."[36] Curiously, some liberals then accused Steinbeck and Kazan of McCarthyism, while at the same time the far right denounced them for dealing with Zapata at all, since all rebels must

[35] Laura Z. Hobson, "Trade Winds," *The Saturday Review*, 35 (March 1, 1952), 6.
[36] Elia Kazan, "Letters to the Editor," *The Saturday Review*, 35 (April 5, 1952), 22.

be Communists. Kazan again replied that, "There was, of course, no such thing as a Communist Party at the time and place where Zapata fought. . . . But there is such a thing as a Communist mentality. We created a figure of this complexion in Fernando," who "typifies the men who use the just grievances of the people for their own ends, who shift and twist their course, betray any friend or principle or promise to get power and keep it." Here then, is Camus's revolutionary, by contrast to Zapata the rebel, whom Kazan calls "a man of individual conscience."[37]

The controversy continued with a criticism of the film by Carleton Beals, an expert on Mexico and one-time instructor to Carranza, who claimed that Zapata's abdication of power was pure fiction. In fact, Zapata repeatedly insisted that he wanted to retire to private life.[38] He emphasized that he could not stand politicians and was afraid, as a politician himself, "of unwittingly betraying the trust his peers and their people had invested in him."[39] According to John Womack, Jr., Zapata did shun power "because it would complicate his original loyalties, but he never really had power to abdicate, or could have had it. Besides, he didn't want power. He wanted an end to harassment from outside, and local peace."[40] He never became President; but in December 1914, he gave up his military power and returned home, rejecting the Villa-Zapata coalition. This is the episode that Steinbeck dramatizes. In reply to Beals, Kazan defended Steinbeck's extensive research, which turned up numerous conflicting accounts of Zapata's mysterious departure from Mexico City. "John had to make choices and he made them with an eye to implementing his interpreta-

[37] *Ibid.*

[38] John Womack, Jr., *Zapata and the Mexican Revolution* (New York: Alfred A. Knopf, 1969), p. 128.

[39] *Ibid.*, p. 205.

[40] Womack, letter to Robert E. Morsberger, April 28, 1973.

tion."[41] Likewise, Camus says of *The Rebel* that his book attempts to "present certain historical data and a working hypothesis. This hypothesis is not the only one possible; moreover, it is far from explaining everything. But it partly explains the direction in which our times are heading."[42]

Steinbeck's interpretation seems to have been reinforced by his earlier visit to Russia; the same year that he began his screenplay, he published *A Russian Journal*. In it he repeatedly condemned the concept of the strong man, objecting to the humorless museum mementos of Lenin and the ubiquitous iconography of Stalin. He recalled that he and photographer Robert Capa "tried to explain our fear of dictatorship, our fear of leaders with too much power, so that our government is designed to keep anyone from getting too much power, or having got it, from keeping it."[43] Steinbeck wanted to avoid political preconceptions and to see the Russian people. He found the Muscovites to be humorless under the weight of ideological dogma; and "after a while the lack of laughter gets under your skin . . ." just as Fernando's sobriety annoyed Eufemio.[44] Eufemio's uninhibited zest resembled the Ukrainians and Georgians, with whom Steinbeck felt at home; like the Mexicans he enjoyed, the Georgians were "fiery, proud, fierce, and gay."[45] By contrast to the official Soviet "heroes of the world," Steinbeck admired the "little people who had been attacked and who had defended themselves successfully."[46]

The final rebel is the artist, in this case Steinbeck him-

[41] Kazan, "Letters to the Editor," *The Saturday Review*, 35 (May 24, 1952), 25, 28.
[42] Camus, *The Rebel*, p. 11.
[43] Steinbeck, *A Russian Journal* (New York: The Viking Press, 1948), p. 57.
[44] *Ibid.*, p. 44.
[45] *Ibid.*, pp. 151–52.
[46] *Ibid.*, pp. 134–35.

self, who noted in *A Russian Journal* that "although Stalin may say that the writer is the architect of the soul, in America the writer is not considered the architect of anything. . . . In nothing is the difference between the Americans and the Soviets so marked as in the attitude, not only toward writers, but of writers toward their system. For in the Soviet Union the writer's job is to encourage, to celebrate, to explain, and in every way to carry forward the Soviet system. Whereas in America, and in England, a good writer is the watch-dog of society. His job is to satirize its silliness, to attack its injustices, to stigmatize its faults. And this is the reason that in America neither society nor government is very fond of writers."[47]

Viva Zapata!'s warnings against power apply equally to the extremists of left-wing revolution and right-wing reaction. The film not only interprets the past but foreshadows events that have since occurred. Philip T. Hartung judged that, "Few historical movies have stated so well the post-revolutionary problem or asked so disturbingly the questions that must be answered about all new leaders."[48] Far from being a digression into Hollywood, Steinbeck's script sums up issues that had long been central to his work. Steinbeck's continuing relevance may be seen in part by the fact that the California grape-pickers who once sang Woody Guthrie's "Tom Joad" now display posters of Emiliano Zapata.

[47] *Ibid.*, p. 164.
[48] Hartung, *Commonweal, loc. cit.*

VIVA ZAPATA!
Twentieth Century-Fox, 1952

Director	Elia Kazan
Producer	Darryl F. Zanuck
Screenplay	John Steinbeck
Director of Photography	Joe MacDonald, A.S.C.
Art Direction	Lyle Wheeler, Leland Fuller
Set Decorations	Thomas Little, Claude Carpenter
Musical Score	Alex North
Musical Direction	Alfred Newman
Film Editor	Barbara McLean, A.C.E.
Wardrobe Direction	Charles Le Maire
Costume Designer	Travilla
Makeup Artist	Ben Nye
Special Photographic Effects	Fred Sersen
Sound	W. D. Flick, Roger Heman
Time: 113 minutes	

Cast

Emiliano Zapata	Marlon Brando
Josefa	Jean Peters
Eufemio	Anthony Quinn
Fernando	Joseph Wiseman
Don Nacio	Arnold Moss
Pancho Villa	Alan Reed
Soldadera	Margo
Pablo	Lou Gilbert
Madero	Harold Gordon
Señora Espejo	Mildred Dunnock
Huerta	Frank Silvera
Aunt	Nina Varela
Señor Espejo	Florenz Ames
Díaz	Fay Roope

Don García	Harry Kingston
Lazaro	Will Kuluva
Zapatista	Bernie Gozier
Colonel Guajardo	Frank De Kova
General Fuentes	Joseph Granby
Fuentes's Wife	Fernanda Elizcu
Innocente	Pedro Regas
Old General	Richard Garrick
Officer	Ross Bagdasarian
Husband	Leonard George
Captain	Abner Biberman
Commanding Officer	Philip Van Zandt
García's Wife	Lisa Fusaro
Nacio's Wife	Belle Mitchell
Soldier	Henry Silva
Eduardo	Guy Thomajan
Rurale	George J. Lewis
Soldiers	Salvador Baguez, Peter Mamakos
Manager	Ric Roman
Senior Officer	Henry Gorden
New General	Nester Paiva
Captain of Rurales	Robert Filmer
Wife	Julia Montoya

A NOTE ON THE SCRIPT

As with most movies, there are a number of changes between the shooting final and the dialogue and details that finally are fixed on the sound track. Steinbeck himself revised the script repeatedly. In the summer of 1950, he wrote to Elia Kazan:

> Last night Elaine read me parts of the script. She liked it very much and I must say I did too. It is a little double-action jewel of a script. But I was glad to hear it again because before it is mouthed by actors, I want to go over the dialogue once more for very small changes. Things like—"For that matter." "As a matter of fact"—in other words all filler words to come out. There isn't much but there is some. I'll want no word in dialogue that has not some definite reference to the story. You said once that you would like this to be some kind of monument. By the same token I would like it to be as tight and terse as possible. It is awfully good but it can be better. Just dialogue—I hear of a dozen places where I can clean it and sharpen it. But outside of that I am very much pleased with it. I truly believe it is a classic example of good film writing. So we'll make it perfect.

Many screenplays are a collaboration between the initial author and the director; some American directors like John Huston, Sam Peckinpah, and Stanley Kubrik often receive credit as co-author of their films. But *Viva Zapata!* is Steinbeck's script. Elia Kazan states: "John and I consulted on the structure and continuity of the script. He wrote it. I made cuts as I shot. But the body of the film, the preponderance of it is a faithful rendering of John's script. No actor rewrote it. I don't go for that.

Zanuck did not rewrite it. He made a few suggestions, several of which we incorporated. But nothing of any moment. The significant changes in the shooting and editing had to do with placing the scenes in locations which we didn't have in mind when we wrote the script. And cuts, cuts, cuts. When a picture tells it, you cut the words. But all John's important words and thoughts arc faithfully in the film."[1]

Most of the changes, as Kazan indicates, are cuts, sometimes of a few words or lines, occasionally of an entire scene or sequence. The most notable cuts are the deletion of the opening title scene of the horsemen and train, a long discussion between Don Nacio and other aristocrats about land ownership, an ambush of a column of horsemen, a conversation between Josefa and her father, in which he complains of Zapata's failure to seize business opportunities, an attempt by the Soldadera to kill Zapata with Pablo's knife, a dialogue between the Charro and Guajardo just before Zapata's assassination, and the entire role of Juana, a camp follower in love with Zapata, who may have been his mistress. Though some of these scenes elaborate on Steinbeck's political philosophy, most of them are expendable; their omission makes the script more taut. Other changes involve reassigning dialogue from one member of a group to another or rearranging some of the word order of a speech. Occasionally, the changes in phrasing sharpen the focus or characterization. For instance, in the audience with Díaz, the shooting final has Lazaro say, "I have a paper from the Spanish crown. I have a paper from the Mexican republic." On the sound track, he says, "We have a paper from the Spanish crown. We have a paper from the Mexican republic." Thus he speaks not for personal gain but for his village. At the end of his first meeting with Zapata, Fernando in the shooting final says, "This is all very con-

[1] Elia Kazan, letter to Robert E. Morsberger, March 29, 1973.

fusing." The revision to "This is all very disorganized" is much more in character for his role of the efficient, relentless ideologue. In the shooting final, Zapata tells Josefa he wants to call on her father "To beg his permission to ask for your hand." The revision, "To ask permission for your hand," is not only more concise, but more in character, since Zapata is not one to beg for anything.

Occasionally, the film makes an addition to the shooting final. The most notable of these is the conclusion to the wedding night, when Zapata persuades Josefa to teach him to read. The shooting final calls for a dissolve after he says, "Begin!!" The film continues, to have her read the opening passage of Genesis, "In the beginning, God created the heaven and the earth," after which she says each phrase slowly for Zapata to repeat.

Elia Kazan says that these changes "seem hardly more than an 'easing' of a certain stiffness or artificiality (conscious and for a purpose) in John's dialogue. They were done on the set and without John's consultation."[2]

It might be argued that since the sound-track dialogue is all that the audience hears, that should be the definitive version. But for readers interested in John Steinbeck's writing, his entire shooting final should be available, even if bits of it were cut or changed in production. After all, very few stage versions use the entire text of a published play. From Shakespeare to Shaw to Tennessee Williams, plays are invariably cut and sometimes even rewritten for performance. The elaborate screen device for *The Glass Menagerie* is never used in production but is always included in the published text. In editing *Twenty Best Film Plays*, John Gassner published complete shooting scripts, despite cuts by the director or the film editor, arguing that "no one reading *Hamlet* is unhappy because the published text does not conform to the abbrevia-

---

[2] Kazan, letter to Morsberger, August 7, 1973.

tions and modifications employed by David Garrick or Sir Harry Irving in their respective productions of the play."[3] However, there can be a number of different stage interpretations from an original text, whereas the movie is fixed in one version. Therefore, in this edition, Steinbeck's shooting final is presented complete with only major cuts for the film indicated by square brackets. The directions for action and camera in the shooting final are Steinbeck's and were not necessarily followed in the filming. Elia Kazan writes that "All shooting script directions have to be adjusted with every day's work. They are not intended by John or any other decent author to be followed rigidly. I didn't. Stage directions are trivia. The words, the spirit, the big images, the theme are the thing."[4]

[3] John Gassner, "The Screenplay as Literature," *Twenty Best Film Plays*, John Gassner and Dudley Nichols, eds. (New York: Crown, 1943), pp. ix–x.
[4] Kazan to Morsberger, March 29, 1973.

[Under the main titles we see these shots:

(a) Long Shot—countryside.

TWO MEN, *one on a* WHITE HORSE, *are riding fast and with intention toward* CAMERA. *Over their ride can be heard the* WAIL *of a* TRAIN WHISTLE, *which seems to increase the tempo of the ride.*

(b) Medium Shot—the Two Horsemen.

The MAN ON THE WHITE HORSE *is in the lead. Both riders wear charro costume.*

(c) A Wayside Stop, or Water Tower—little more than a whistle stop, where the train stops to pick up passengers.

A number of white-clad PEASANTS *are waiting expectantly. The* TWO HORSEMEN *ride into scene, and dismount.*

The Titles Stop.

OTHER HORSEMAN (*to the* MAN ON THE WHITE HORSE): You're wasting your time, my brother. Nothing will come of this—nothing at all.
Over scene comes the SOUND *of the* TRAIN WHISTLE. *The* PEASANTS *and the* TWO HORSEMEN *look off toward the sound. The* MAN ON THE WHITE HORSE *turns back to his brother (the* OTHER HORSEMAN*), hands him the reins of the* WHITE HORSE, *and walks toward the group of waiting* PEASANTS.]

Fade out

3

Fade in:

Gate to Palace, Shooting toward Palace

The white-clad PEASANTS *whom we saw waiting for the train are standing at the gate. Among them we recognize the* MAN ON THE WHITE HORSE. SOLDIERS *guard the gateway.*

Medium Shot—Group of Peasants at Gate

ONE OF THE PEASANTS *produces a paper which is scrutinized by the* SOLDIERS, *who then proceed to search each member of the party for weapons. From one they take a knife, from another a gun, etc., and hand them to another* SOLDIER *who stands in the doorway of the guardhouse.*

Interior, Guardhouse

There are rows of nails on the wall. The SOLDIER *in the doorway now turns, hangs the peasants' weapons on the nails—indicating that it is common practice to relieve callers of their weapons and retain them until they leave the palace. For the most part, the peasants' weapons consist of long, murderous-looking sheath knives.*

At the Gate

The MAN ON THE WHITE HORSE *is standing before the* SOLDIER *who takes his weapon and hands it to the* SOLDIER *in the doorway. Immediately behind the* MAN ON THE WHITE HORSE *is a* SLIGHT MAN (PABLO), *who gives up his weapon—a short knife. The* SOLDIER *stares at the knife in disbelief.*

Insert—the Knife, a very inoffensive little weapon.

Back to Scene

The SOLDIER, *with a grin, hands the knife back to* PABLO. *The* MAN ON THE WHITE HORSE *looks at the knife in amusement, and* SAYS *to* PABLO:

4

THE MAN ON THE WHITE HORSE: When are you going
to get a *real* knife?
All the OTHER PEASANTS *smile.*
Now all the PEASANTS *have been searched, and passed.
A* SOLDIER *gestures to them to follow him. As they
start after him—*

Dissolve to:
Interior, Audience Room in Palace
   An USHER, *in formal attire, admits the* PEASANTS, *then
   exits. An* ATTENDANT, *with a card and pencil, comes
   to them.*
ATTENDANT: *Your names, please.*
   After they have given their names, the PEASANTS *look
   around the room. On one side there is a large throne-
   like chair. Prominently evident on one wall is a picture
   of* DÍAZ, *in all his glory. The* PEASANTS *group before
   this picture and all stare at it.*
VOICE *(offstage)*: Good morning, my children.

Full Shot—The Audience Room
   *It is bare, with no chairs except one behind a big desk.
   The* PEASANT DELEGATION, *standing before* DÍAZ'S
   picture, turns toward the VOICE. *Standing in the door-
   way is* DÍAZ, *the President of Mexico. He looks at them
   briefly, then he moves briskly to his desk, and sits. The*
   ATTENDANT *gives him the card with the names of the
   delegation.* DÍAZ *studies it for a moment. Then:*
DÍAZ *(with a gesture)*: Come closer, come closer.
   They shuffle in toward his desk.

Medium Shot—Diaz and Delegation
DÍAZ: Now, then, my children . . . what's the problem
you have brought me?
   The DELEGATES *look at one another, hesitate as to who
   should speak first. (The* MAN ON THE WHITE HORSE
   remains in the background.)

5

DÍAZ: Well, one of you has to tell . . . you must have come for something.

LAZARO *(a* DELEGATE; *in simple agreement)*: Yes, my President. We have come for something.

DÍAZ *(looking at* ANOTHER DELEGATE*)*: Well, you—you tell me.

FIRST DELEGATE: You know that field, that field with the big white rock in the middle just south of Anencuilco. . . .

SECOND DELEGATE *(a prepared speech)*: My President, our delegation—

PABLO *(interrupting with great violence)*: They took our land away!

DÍAZ: Who took your land away . . . ? My children, when you make accusations, be certain that you have all your facts. Who took your land away?

DELEGATES *(together)*: The big estate there! It's bigger than a kingdom! They have taken the green valley! They have left us only the rocky hillsides! There's a new fence—with barbed wire. We can't feed our cows.

FIRST DELEGATE: You know those three houses by the white rock? They burned those.

SECOND DELEGATE: They're planting sugar cane in our corn land.

DÍAZ: Can you prove you own this field?

LAZARO *(more calmly)*: Our village has owned this land since before history. *(holding up worn leather case)* I have a paper from the Spanish crown. I have a paper from the Mexican republic.

DÍAZ: If this is true, you have no problem. *(pause)* My children, the courts will settle this. I will send you to my personal attorney. But before you see him, I urge you: Find the boundary stones. And check them against your grants and titles. Verify the boundaries. Facts—facts—

The DELEGATES *break into expression of acquiescence and gratitude.*

DÍAZ *(continuing)*: Now! I have many other matters to

6

attend to. *(with a smile)* I have been your President for thirty-four years. It is not easy being President.

ELDERLY DELEGATE: Thank you, my President.

Wider Angle

> *They all back away, leaving the* MAN ON THE WHITE HORSE *standing alone. He just stands there unmoving, looking at the* PRESIDENT *with calculating eyes. The* OTHER DELEGATES, *seeing that he has not moved, stop. When he* SPEAKS, *his face is expressionless but his* VOICE *is soft and pleasant.*

THE MAN ON THE WHITE HORSE: We can't verify the boundaries, my President. The land is fenced, guarded by armed men. At this moment they're planting sugar cane in our corn fields.

DÍAZ *(starting to speak)*: The courts—

> *The* MAN ON THE WHITE HORSE *holds up his hand with instinctive authority.*

THE MAN ON THE WHITE HORSE: With your permission— the courts! Do you know any land suit that's ever been won by country people?

DÍAZ: Has your land been taken?

THE MAN ON THE WHITE HORSE: My father's land, my President, was taken long ago.

> DÍAZ *looks at him a moment. Then he turns and* SPEAKS *past him to the* OTHER VILLAGERS.

DÍAZ: My children. I am your father, your protector, I am of your blood. Believe me these things take time, you must have patience.

THE MAN ON THE WHITE HORSE: My President, as you know we make our tortillas of corn, not patience. And patience will not cross an armed and guarded fence. To do as you suggest—to verify those boundaries—we need your authority to cross that fence. . . .

DÍAZ: I cannot possibly exercise such authority.

THE MAN ON THE WHITE HORSE: But you advised it. . . .

DÍAZ: I can only advise.

7

THE MAN ON THE WHITE HORSE: Then naturally, my
President, we will do as you advise. Thank you, my Presi-
dent. *(he bows)* With your permission?
*And only as he turns is there the suggestion of a smile
in his eyes. He starts for the door, the* OTHER DELE-
GATES *going along.*

Close Shot—Díaz

*His face shows a suspicion that he has been had. Sud-
denly he calls out.*
DÍAZ: You!

Medium Shot—Group at Door

Just inside the exit door the MAN ON THE WHITE HORSE
*stops and half turns. There is a natural insolence about
him.*
THE MAN ON THE WHITE HORSE: Yes, my President?
DÍAZ'S VOICE: What's your name?
THE MAN ON THE WHITE HORSE: Zapata.

Another Angle—Including Díaz and Zapata

DÍAZ: What is it . . . ?
ZAPATA *(pronouncing it carefully)*: Emiliano Zapata.
*DÍAZ stares at him briefly, then, for his benefit he care-
fully writes on a pad, or card:*

*Insert—Díaz's Hand, circling the name "Zapata" on the card
which the* Attendant *gave him when he entered the room.*

Back to Scene

DÍAZ looks up at ZAPATA *to see if he notices the threat
involved in the circled name.* ZAPATA *stares back at
him. They look at each other for a moment, in a kind
of combat; then* ZAPATA *turns, walks toward the* GROUP
AT THE DOOR, *leaving DÍAZ looking after him.*

8

Lap Dissolve to:
Exterior, a Fenced Field in Morelos—near Ayala

> *A large group of* VILLAGERS, MEN, WOMEN, *and* CHIL-
> DREN, *stand at the fence. Among them is a* BOY *who
> carries a picture of the Virgin of Guadalupe mounted
> on a stick. A* VILLAGE ELDER *holds in his hand the
> leather case we have established as containing the vil-
> lage titles and records. There is also a small* GROUP ON
> HORSEBACK, *among them* EMILIANO *and* EUFEMIO
> ZAPATA.

Close Shot—Emiliano and Eufemio

EMILIANO *(to* EUFEMIO*)*: Cut the fence.
EUFEMIO: Yes, my brother.

The People as they go through the fence.

> *Most of the* WOMEN *remain outside. The* LEADERS *look
> for the first boundary marker.*

*Close Shot—the Village Elder, holding the documents, and
studying a map.*

VILLAGE ELDER: The old boundary stone should be about
here.

Wider Angle

> *An* INDIAN *reaches down, picks up a piece of brick
> with mortar still clinging to its side.*
INDIAN: Here's a piece of it.
> *An* OLD INDIAN *brings forth the picture of the Virgin
> of Guadalupe, plants it in the ground. The* PEOPLE
> *pile stones about the picture. Suddenly over scene
> comes the* SOUND *of a* BUGLE—*a* SHRILL BLAST *which
> freezes the* PEOPLE *in the field. They stand rigid for
> a moment, then look off toward:*

Long Shot

FORTY MOUNTED RURALES *trot over a hill in the distance. Their* BUGLE BLOWS *again. They ride at full charge toward the* GROUP.

Full Shot—Inside the Fenced Field

EMILIANO *and* EUFEMIO *ride in,* YELLING: "Go!" "Run!" "Get out!" "Go through the fence!" *as they begin to herd the* PEOPLE *toward the hole in the fence. Suddenly there is a* BURST OF MACHINE-GUN FIRE.

Group at Hole in Fence

Struggling to get through the fence, are cut down by the MACHINE-GUN FIRE.

Emiliano

He whirls about to locate the machine gun.

The Machine Gun

It has been set up and is being worked by FIVE MEN. WE ARE SHOOTING PAST *the* GUN CREW, OVER *the sights. Suddenly the* FEEDER *grasps the* GUNNER *by the arm and points. The* GUNNER *first looks and then swings his gun.* CAMERA SWINGS *too, and still over the sights we see* TWO HORSEMEN *coming zigzag at the machine gun. The* GUNNER FIRES.

Machine Gun and Crew

Now the HORSEMEN (EMILIANO *and* EUFEMIO) *are on them.* EMILIANO *carries a* reata *(rope) and as his horse leaps the gun he drops the noose over the barrel.* WE STAY *with the* MACHINE-GUN CREW. *The noose tightens and the gun is yanked with great force out of their hands*

Long Shot—Rurales

The RURALES *are riding over the* PEOPLE *who are trying to get through the hole in the fence. The* PEOPLE *are scattered, falling down, running, tripping, etc.*

Medium Shot—Captain of Rurales and Some of His Men

The CAPTAIN *points toward* EMILIANO.
CAPTAIN: There he is! That's the one in our orders! That's Zapata!
They start toward him.

Group of Rurales at Fence

EMILIANO—*all alone*—*rides down on the* RURALES *and disappears into the melee. His* HORSEMEN, *seeing what he has done, charge in after him. There is a temporary diversion, during which a good number of* VILLAGE PEOPLE *get through the fence.*

Close Shot—Emiliano

Suddenly he leaps to the back of a RURALE'S HORSE, *holds the* MAN'S *arms, and drives his spurs into the* HORSE'S *flanks.*

Wider Angle, as the frightened Horse bursts clear of the melee.

The RURALE *falls from the* HORSE. *In the background we see the remnants of the* VILLAGERS *taking advantage of the momentary diversion* EMILIANO *has created, escaping through the fence.*

Medium Shot—Captain of Rurales as the Rurales surround him for further orders.

He points off toward the fleeing ZAPATA, *and orders his* MEN *after him. They whirl their* HORSES, *ride off.*

Long Shot—Emiliano riding away.

He suddenly seems to vanish in a dense growth of chaparal and mesquite. The moment he disappears, the RURALES RIDE INTO THE SHOT. *They don't know where he has gone.*

Medium Shot—Captain of Rurales as he hurriedly orders his men off in different directions, to try to find Emiliano.
Fade out

Fade in:
Long Shot—Precipitous and Savage Mountains—Day
Climbing up a steep footpath is a YOUNG MAN.

Close Shot—of the Young Man, Fernando Aguirre

He is dressed in rumpled city clothes. He is literally soaked with sweat. He wears a high collar, and boots which come up over his trouser legs. He carries his coat over one arm, a straw hat, and a brief case in the other hand. Hanging from his belt is an 1892 American model typewriter. He is pooped. Suddenly he stops, cups his hands, and SHOUTS.
FERNANDO: Zapata. . . . Emiliano Zapata . . . !
Receiving no answer he trudges on.

A Cave Behind a Big Rock

*We go to a figure (*PABLO*), whom we should remember as one of the* HORSEMEN *in the boundary-marking scene. . . . He has just been awakened by the* SHOUT. *Nearby, the mouth of the cave. In front of it is the* CARCASS *of a hung deer in the process of being jerked, laid out on its own skin. Beside the cave* THREE HORSES *are tied up short. One, a* STALLION, *is fighting its halter.*

A WOMAN OF THE COUNTRY, *still half girl, with a kind of savage animal beauty, is crouched over the fire cooking strips of venison. We will call her the* SOL-DADERA.

A SHOT SOUNDS. . . . PABLO *gets heavily to his feet and strolls to a big rock and looks around it.*

*A Little Crevice Overlooking Trail—Emiliano and Eufemio
lying there.*

> *Their clothes are ragged. They have the wary look of
> hunted animals.* EUFEMIO *has just* FIRED *his rifle.*
> PABLO *comes into scene.*

EUFEMIO *(looking down trail)*: He's still coming.

EMILIANO: Who do you think he is?

PABLO: A stranger . . . look at his clothes.

EUFEMIO *(to* EMILIANO*)*: Shall I kill him, little brother?

EMILIANO: Shoot in front of him again. . . .

PABLO: Careful. Don't hit him.

EUFEMIO: When I want to hit them, I hit them. When
I want to miss them, I miss them.

PABLO: A man has been known to die of a close miss.

> EUFEMIO *carefully draws his carbine up and sights. . . .
> Shot and* WHINE *of a bullet.* FERNANDO *stops. Then
> holding up his hat and brief case ahead of him in a
> gesture of peace, he continues walking.*

Crevice—Emiliano, Eufemio, and Pablo

PABLO: He's crazy. It's not nice to kill crazy people.

EUFEMIO: Shall I try him again, a little closer. . . .

PABLO: A little closer! How can you come closer?

Close Shot—Fernando

FERNANDO: Zapata! Emiliano Zapata!

Crevice—Emiliano, Eufemio, and Pablo

PABLO: Maybe he has a message. . . .

EUFEMIO: Maybe it's a trap. Why don't we kill him?
It's so much easier instead of so much worry. Besides,
what does it cost? One little bullet.

EMILIANO: No.

> *He stands up and faces the approaching* FERNANDO.

EMILIANO *(calling to him)*: What do you want?

15

Wider Angle—Crevice, as Fernando comes in to them.

EUFEMIO *covers him with his gun.* FERNANDO *turns to* PABLO, *holds out his hand.*

FERNANDO *(introducing himself)*: Fernando Aguirre.

PABLO *(taking his hand)*: Pablo Gómez.

FERNANDO: I'm looking for Emiliano Zapata.

EUFEMIO *(answering for* PABLO*)*: He's not here!

FERNANDO: His friends sent me.

EUFEMIO: Who are his friends?

FERNANDO: The people of the village.

EUFEMIO: He's not here!

EMILIANO *gestures to* EUFEMIO *to search* FERNANDO. *He goes over his pockets, and legs of trousers.*

FERNANDO: I have no weapons.

EUFEMIO *(points to typewriter)*: What's this?

PABLO: It's a writing machine.

FERNANDO: Yes—the sword of the mind.

EUFEMIO: I thought you had no weapons.

EUFEMIO *lifts it as though to smash it on a rock.*

FERNANDO *(suddenly, with great violence)*: Don't you dare break that! *(*EUFEMIO *pauses)* Don't you dare. Put it down!!!

EUFEMIO *looks at his brother.* FERNANDO *has ferocity.* EMILIANO *respects this.*

EMILIANO: Put it down.

FERNANDO *(with sudden anger)*: You're Emiliano Zapata. I have news of Madero, the leader of the fight against Díaz. Give me some water.

EMILIANO: Why do you come to me?   .

FERNANDO *(fiercely)*: Give me some water!! I want to talk to you.

EMILIANO *turns, starts off toward their camp.*

Exterior, Camp—near Cave

The FOUR MEN *come in.* EMILIANO *hands* FERNANDO *a gourd of water, then crosses over to his* STALLION.

16

PABLO *crouches at the fire near the* SOLDADERA. *He holds out his hand. She puts a piece of meat in it. He drops it because it is hot, and shakes his fingers. The* SOLDADERA *picks up the meat, dusts it off, blows on it, and puts it back in his hand.* FERNANDO *drinks from the gourd.*

Close Shot—Eufemio, watching Fernando.

Close Shot—Pablo, watching Fernando.

Close Shot—Emiliano pretending to be engrossed in his Horse, but at the same time stealing glances at Fernando.

Medium Shot, taking in all Four Men.

FERNANDO *finishes drinking, looks at the other* THREE MEN, *who quickly drop their eyes.*
FERNANDO *(to* EMILIANO*)*: I want to talk to you.
EMILIANO *(from the side of the* STALLION*)*: Talk.
FERNANDO: I want you to listen.
EMILIANO: Talk.
FERNANDO *picks up his brief case and goes over to* EMILIANO.

Eufemio, Pablo, and the Soldadera at the fire.

As they talk, they watch FERNANDO *and* EMILIANO, *who are about twenty feet away.*
EUFEMIO *(worried)*: It's so much harder to kill a man after you once talk to him. Even a few words.
PABLO: Shsh! Listen.

Fernando and Emiliano

FERNANDO *takes out a packet of clippings, selects one which has on it a photograph of* Madero. *He starts reading from it.*
FERNANDO: "The despotism of Porfirio Díaz is unbearable. For more than thirty-four years he has ruled with the hand of a ruthless tyrant."

EMILIANO *takes the newspaper from him and studies* MADERO's *picture.*

Insert—Newspaper Clipping, showing picture of Madero.
Back to Scene

EMILIANO *looks intently at the picture. A* COYOTE
HOWLS; *the* WHITE STALLION *is restive.*

EMILIANO *(gently, to the* HORSE*)*: Steady. Pretty soon
now, Blanco.

FERNANDO: Listen—*(reads from another newspaper)*
"The true meaning of democracy has long been forgotten
in Mexico. Elections are a farce. The people have no
voice in the Government. The control of the country is
in the hands of one man and those he has appointed to
carry out his orders."

PABLO's VOICE *(calling across)*: Who wrote that?

FERNANDO: Francisco Madero.

EMILIANO *(still studying the photograph)*: I like his
face.

*He folds the newspaper clipping and puts it into his
pocket.*

FERNANDO *(reading)*: "If we are to bring back to Mexico
the freedom that goes with democracy we must unite to
drive this tyrant from office. We will blow the little
flames into one great fire!"

Close Shot—Eufemio and Pablo at the Fire

EUFEMIO *(to* PABLO*)*: Who is Madero?

Close Shot—Fernando

He turns toward them as he overhears EUFEMIO's *question.*

FERNANDO: Leader of the fight against Díaz.

Wide Angle—Group

FERNANDO *walks over to the fire, to* EUFEMIO *and*
PABLO.

PABLO: Where is he?

FERNANDO: Right now he's in a part of the United States. Texas.

EUFEMIO: A fine place to lead a fight against Díaz!

FERNANDO *(fiercely)*: From Texas he's been making preparations. Now he's ready to move. He's sending out many people like me to spread the word and search out leaders in other parts of Mexico. *(looks toward* EMILI-ANO*)* I was sent to the State of Morelos.

Emiliano

> *He's been listening intently, but now he covers up by busying himself with his* WHITE STALLION.

EMILIANO: I don't like to tie him close. But the smell of a mare came in on the wind this morning. He's restless. So am I.

Full Shot—Featuring Fernando

> *He reacts to the speech, and looks at* EMILIANO *penetratingly. Then:*

FERNANDO: The people in your town told me—

EUFEMIO *(interrupting)*: Don't believe what people tell you. Eat!!!

> *The* SOLDADERA *takes a piece of the venison from the fire, blows on it, hands it to* FERNANDO. *Now* PABLO *moves toward* EMILIANO *with affected casualness. . . .*

PABLO: Let me see that split hoof. . . .

Pablo and Emiliano bending over the Horse's *hoof.*

EMILIANO *(eagerly)*: Madero!

PABLO: Yes. You remember I once read about him to you from the newspaper. . . .

EMILIANO *(with the sudden violence of frustration)*: You promised to teach me to read!!

PABLO *(placatingly)*: I will. . . . I will. . . . Let's ask this man more about Madero. Maybe he's got a letter.

19

EMILIANO: Anybody can write a letter, even you. . . . I'd like to look at Madero's eyes. . . .

PABLO: Then go—go to wherever he is and talk to him. . . .

EMILIANO: No I can't. Not now.

PABLO: Why not? *(no answer.* PABLO *speaks a little bitterly)* I know why. . . .

EMILIANO *(bending close to him)*: I want you to go to Madero and look in his face and tell me what you see. . . .

PABLO: Me! He's in Texas. . . .

EMILIANO: Well, go to Texas.

PABLO: How far is it?

EMILIANO: Who knows? Go and see.

He takes out the newspaper clipping and looks at it again.

PABLO: I've never been out of our state. . . .

EMILIANO: Now you will be. . . . I can't go now. I want you to go. Look at Madero and see whether we can trust him. . . . A picture is only a picture.

PABLO: When do you want me to go?

EMILIANO: Now. . . . When else?

PABLO *still hesitates.*

EMILIANO: Now!! Cinch up.

Wider Angle as Pablo Mounts.

EMILIANO *goes to the fire . . . takes hunks of cooked meat and stuffs them in* PABLO's *saddlebag.*

Close Shot—Emiliano and Pablo

EMILIANO *(whispering)*: If you like what you see in his face, tell him we recognize him as the leader of the Revolution. Tell him about our troubles here.

Full Shot

PABLO *kicks his* HORSE *and rides off.* EMILIANO *goes to the fire and picks up a piece of meat and chews, thinking.*

20

FERNANDO: Where did he go?

EMILIANO: I don't know. He didn't say.

Suddenly he turns to his HORSE, *quickly mounts, and rides away in an opposite direction.*

FERNANDO *(amazed)*: Now *he's* going! Where's he going?

EUFEMIO *(same tone as* EMILIANO*)*: I don't know—he didn't say!

FERNANDO: What's the matter with him?

EUFEMIO *(turning toward his* HORSE*)*: A woman. What else? *(he mounts the* HORSE*)*

FERNANDO: Where are *you* going?

EUFEMIO *(shrugging)*: What else?!

He turns his HORSE, *starts after* EMILIANO.

FERNANDO *(*CALLING AFTER *him, indicating the* SOLDADERA*)*: What about her?

Close Shot—Eufemio

He CALLS *back over his shoulder.*

EUFEMIO: She'll take care of herself. . . .

He disappears.

Close-up—Fernando

looking off after EUFEMIO. *He takes out his handkerchief, mops his brow.*

FERNANDO *(to the* SOLDADERA*)*: This is all very confusing.

Wider Angle

He turns toward her and stops suddenly as he sees she is not there. He looks around for her—sees:

Long Shot

of the SOLDADERA, *disappearing down the trail.*

21

Close-up—Fernando

He lets out an exasperated sigh, picks up his type-writer, prepares to leave.

Dissolve to:
Exterior, Street in Ayala—Night

Two Women, *black shawls concealing their heads and lower faces, hurry down the narrow street. They pass a* Policeman.

Policeman: Good evening, Señora Espejo; good evening, Señorita. . . .

He moves on. As he passes a corner, around the building appear Emiliano *and* Eufemio, *looking after him. They don't want the* Policeman *to see them. They look down the street after the* Two Women. *Then covering their noses with their serapes, they move cautiously after the* Women.

Exterior, the Church

as Josefa Espejo *and her* Aunt *enter. As the door closes behind them,* Emiliano *and* Eufemio *come into scene, quickly enter the church.*

Interior, Church

It is provincial and rather dark and deserted. The Two Women *make their duties, and sit down.*

Rear of Church

Emiliano *and* Eufemio *have entered, and stand looking off toward the* Women. *They, too, make their duties, then start past the screen which is around the fount. As they do,* Emiliano *taps* Eufemio *on the shoulder, points to the rifle he is carrying. Both men stand their rifles in the corner. Then they separate, one going down one aisle, the other, the other.*

EMILIANO *moves in beside* JOSEFA, EUFEMIO *on the other side of the* AUNT. *Simultaneously they are beside the women.*

Close Shot—Group

EMILIANO *(to* JOSEFA*)*: I must talk to you. . . .

The AUNT *turns her head, with an* EXCLAMATION—*and instantly finds her arms pinned to her side and her mouth covered by* EUFEMIO'S *hand.* JOSEFA *looks at her* AUNT, *sees she is held tightly by* EUFEMIO, *then turns to* EMILIANO.

JOSEFA: The Rurales are after you!

EMILIANO: I know, Josefa, I have risked my life to come here. . . . When may I call on your father?

JOSEFA: What for?

EMILIANO: To beg his permission to ask for your hand.

JOSEFA: Oh no! Don't do it!

EMILIANO: Why not?

JOSEFA: Don't do it.

EMILIANO: What's wrong with me?

JOSEFA: That's not it. What would be wrong with me if I married you?

EMILIANO: What do you mean?

JOSEFA: I have no intention of ending up washing clothes in a ditch and patting tortillas like an Indian.

EMILIANO: Who says that?

JOSEFA: Sh! My father.

EMILIANO *(his* VOICE RISING *steadily and fiercely to a crescendo)*: My mother was a Salazar! Zapatas were chieftains here when *your* grandfather lived in a cave!

JOSEFA: Shsh! We're in church. Well, you're not chieftains *now*! You have no money, no land. Without luck you'll probably be in jail by tomorrow.

EMILIANO: It happens I have been offered an important position by Don Nacio de la Torre y Mier.

23

JOSEFA (*her* VOICE RISING): Don Nacio de la Torre does not employ fugitives from the law!

EMILIANO: If I accept his offer, he will have the charges against me dismissed!

JOSEFA: Why in the world would Don Nacio need anyone like *you*?? Why??

EMILIANO: Apparently you have not heard that I am the best judge of horses in the country. You are the only one who has not heard this. I worked for him for years. I bought every horse in his stable for him. When I have not helped Don Nacio buy his horses, it is later discovered that they have—(*almost* SHOUTING)—five legs!

EUFEMIO, *who has been listening with interest, has let his hand slip from the* AUNT'*s mouth.*

AUNT: What a conceited monkey!

EUFEMIO'*s hand comes back to place.*

JOSEFA: Well, I notice you haven't accepted this offer. And now if you'll allow my aunt to breathe we'll continue our devotions. . . . (*there's a pause*)

EMILIANO: Then I will have to take you by force—

JOSEFA: By force? I would not prevent you. I would go with you because I couldn't prevent you. . . . But sooner or later you will go to sleep. . . .

EMILIANO: What's that got to do with it?

JOSEFA (*takes a steel pin from her hair—holds it up in front of his eyes and repeats*): Sooner or later you will go to sleep. . . .

EMILIANO: You'd never do that. A respectable girl like you.

JOSEFA: Yes I would! Because I *am* a respectable girl. A respectable girl wants to live a safe life— Protected! Uneventful! Without surprises! And preferably with a rich man.

EMILIANO (*really deeply shocked*): You don't mean that. . . !

JOSEFA: I do. Come back when you can offer me that. (*turns to* AUNT) He's going to let you go now. Don't scream. The police are after him. . . . *(now to* EUFEMIO*)* Let her go. . . . *(*EUFEMIO *doesn't)*

EMILIANO *(abruptly)*: Let her go. . . . *(*EUFEMIO *does so)* I'll be back. Don't think I won't be back.

The TWO MEN *rise, quickly and quietly slip away from the* WOMEN, *go to the rear door of the church.* JOSEFA *and her* AUNT *look at each other. Suddenly and unexpectedly, and even to her own considerable surprise the* AUNT SAYS:

AUNT: I like him.

JOSEFA *(shocked, surprised)*: You do?

AUNT: I mean—he's a terrible man . . . a fugitive—a criminal!

JOSEFA: I like him too. . . .

Dissolve to:
Exterior, Large Courtyard

walled on three sides. Along one side, watching, are some poverty-stricken PEOPLE. *The fourth side is the entrance to a magnificent stable. In the center of the courtyard,* FIVE ARABIAN HORSES *are being led in a circle. Each* HORSE *is led by an* INDIAN, *and as they lead the* HORSES, *they* TALK SOFTLY *among themselves in the Aztec language. The* HORSES *are being shown off to* DON NACIO DE LA TORRE, *who is seated in a chair. Beside him stands* THE MANAGER *and slightly behind him on the other side is* EMILIANO.

[*Medium Shot—Don Nacio, Emiliano, and Manager*

THE MANAGER: Directly from Arabia, pure blood line. I don't know why my master is willing to sell them, Don Nacio.

DON NACIO: I think they're beautiful *(turns to* EMILIANO; *in a* WHISPER*)* I don't trust his master. Do you trust the horses?

EMILIANO *has been listening to the* TALK *of the* INDIANS *who lead the* HORSES. *His attention is pulled back.*

26

EMILIANO: They're all right.

DON NACIO *(preparing to get up)*: Well . . . if you think so. *(turns to* MANAGER*)* My major-domo has the best eye for a horse in the south of Mexico.

EMILIANO *puts his hand on* DON NACIO*'s arm.*

EMILIANO: Where are the others?

THE MANAGER: What others?

EMILIANO: Weren't there ten in the shipment from Arabia?

THE MANAGER *(stumbling)*: Oh, I didn't think you'd want to see them, Don Nacio.

DON NACIO: Oh, but we do!

THE MANAGER: Besides, they're not for sale.

DON NACIO: We'll look at them.

THE MANAGER: Certainly . . . this way. *(he starts out)*

DON NACIO *(*WHISPERING *to* EMILIANO*)*: How did you know there were ten?

EMILIANO: The Indians. They were talking in their own tongue.

As they start after THE MANAGER, EMILIANO SPEAKS *to the* INDIANS *in the Aztec language. They* LAUGH.

DON NACIO: I forgot you knew Aztec. Our Spanish is fine in the cities, but in the country I've often wished I could understand the Indians.

The INDIANS LAUGH *again to themselves.* DON NACIO *looks at* EMILIANO.

DON NACIO: I must say you look very well. You take naturally to being a gentleman.]

Close Shot—Bowl, showing hands breaking eggs in the bowl.

Another hand puts a sponge into the egg mixture and the CAMERA RISES *with the sponge and we see an* IN-DIAN *sponging the eggs into the coat of a* HORSE *tied to the outside of a box stall.* CAMERA PULLS BACK *and we see that we are in the magnificent stables. The floor is cobbled in tiny stones set in designs, black and red. Along one wall are luxurious carriages. To the rear are box stalls. The building is of stone, the stalls and mangers of marble. A stream of clear, fresh water runs in a trench down the middle.*

Into the scene walk THE MANAGER, DON NACIO *and* EMILIANO. *The first two are looking at the* HORSE, *which is being polished. A* LITTLE GIRL, *sitting beside the* WOMAN *who is breaking the eggs, with a quick thievish gesture, dips her finger into the mixture and puts it into her mouth. Her* MOTHER, *seeing that* EMILIANO *has noticed this, slaps her hand. The* LITTLE GIRL *puts down her head in shame.* EMILIANO *also looks away in shame.*

THE MANAGER *(to the* INDIAN *who is wielding the sponge)*: Rub it in . . . rub it harder. *(to* DON NACIO*)* They're so lazy. . . . Luncheon is ready now. *(he moves toward the door)*

EMILIANO *(gesturing towards the* HORSE *being sponged; softly to* DON NACIO*)*: That's the best of the lot. Let's look at the others.

THE MANAGER: So lazy! If they're not stealing, they're asleep. If they are awake, they're drunk.

DON NACIO *(*LOUDLY*)*: Let's look at the others!

THE MANAGER *(*LOUD*)*: But luncheon is served!

DON NACIO *(*LOUD *and* STRONG*)*: It can wait!

DON NACIO *and* EMILIANO, *trailed by* THE MANAGER, *walk down the line of box stalls,* CAMERA MOVING *with them.* EMILIANO *pauses and looks into a box stall.* THE OTHERS *walk on a few paces, then turn and look back at* EMILIANO. *They step back to him, look in through the bars of the stall.*

Close Shot—Manger

A LITTLE BOY *is shrinking into the hay at the bottom of the manger, attempting to hide. He's been caught in the act of stealing the* HORSES' *food. His hand and mouth are caked with mash.* THE MANAGER *reaches in, grabs the* BOY, *yanks him out of the manger.*

Group Shot at Manger

DON NACIO: What is it?

THE MANAGER: Stealing! You see? You can't turn your back on them! Even the *horses'* food!

He slashes at the BOY *with his quirt. The second time he raises his hand,* EMILIANO *grabs his wrist.*

EMILIANO: Stop it.

THE MANAGER: They steal everything!

He tears his wrist loose and slashes again at the CHILD. EMILIANO *reverses his* charro *whip and knocks* THE MANAGER *to the floor. He means to kill him! As he raises the* charro *whip again,* DON NACIO *throws himself at him and knocks him off balance.*

DON NACIO: Stop it! . . . Emiliano . . . stop it!

He forces EMILIANO *outside.*

Exterior, the Stable

EMILIANO *is standing still, trembling.* DON NACIO *paces around him.*

DON NACIO: When I had the charges against you dismissed you promised—

EMILIANO: I know.

DON NACIO: It wasn't easy.

EMILIANO: I know.

DON NACIO: I don't want to regret it. Emiliano, I told you. Violence is no good.

EMILIANO *(suddenly reverting)*: Then why does *he* use it?

DON NACIO *(stopping him with his arm)*: You're full of anger.

EMILIANO: That boy was hungry.

DON NACIO: Calm down, calm down! *(lighting a cigar)* Look, Emiliano. . . . You're a clever man and an able man. You might even be an important man, have money and property, be respected. That's what you told me you wanted. . . . Do you want it or don't you?

EMILIANO *(quietly)*: He was hungry.

29

DON NACIO: Are you responsible for everybody? You can't be the conscience of the whole world.

Wider Angle

taking in a ragged group of INDIANS *watching the* TWO MEN. *They've seen and understood. One of them makes a joke in his own language and the rest burst into* LAUGHTER. EMILIANO LAUGHS *too, in spite of himself. The air is cleared.*

EMILIANO *(to* DON NACIO*)*: Have you another cigar?

DON NACIO: The most civilized thing about you is your taste for good cigars. *(the* INDIANS LAUGH *again)* What was the joke?

EMILIANO: Just Indian talk. . . . They're just Indians.

He bursts out LAUGHING *again.*

DON NACIO: I'm going to prescribe for you. You need that wife. Have you ever spoken to Josefa's father?

EMILIANO: No.

DON NACIO: Why not?

EMILIANO: I don't like him and he doesn't like me.

DON NACIO: In the world of business, few people like each other, but they have to get along—or there wouldn't be any business. . . . Emiliano, look, now you have a position—clothes—go to Señor Espejo—tell him I'm your patron. Make your peace with him. *(warningly)* And don't forget that the President has drawn a circle around your name. You must behave. *(he points to* THE MANAGER *standing at a distance)* Now you'd better start practicing. Go over and apologize to him.

EMILIANO *hesitates, then turns and stalks toward* THE MANAGER. THE MANAGER *moves away.*

EMILIANO *(*SHOUTING *after him)*: I apologize!

THE MANAGER *(from a safe distance)*: Accepted, accepted.

EMILIANO *(turning to* DON NACIO*)*: Was that all right. . . ?

DON NACIO LAUGHS. *Then stops as he notices that*

EMILIANO *is suddenly intent on something. He turns and looks and sees among the* INDIANS *in the background behind him a* STRANGER *who walks toward* EMILIANO. *It is* PABLO.

DON NACIO: Do you know him?

EMILIANO: Yes. He's a friend. He's been away.

Without another word he leaves DON NACIO *and walks toward* PABLO.

Close Shot—Pablo and Emiliano

PABLO *is dressed as usual, in a worn brown* charro *costume, except that, at the throat, instead of a scarf or string tie, he wears a celluloid collar and a bright necktie.*

EMILIANO *(pointing to collar and tie)*: What's that. . . ?

PABLO *(simply)*: Texas!

EMILIANO LAUGHS. *They embrace warmly. . . . Suddenly he sees something.*

FERNANDO *is standing, as if waiting, at one side. He looks at* EMILIANO. *Smiles.*

Dissolve to:
[*Long Shot—Road—Day*

The road leads up to a ford of a small stream. FOUR HORSEMEN *ride up and dismount, to let their* HORSES *drink in a stream. It's apparent from the dust on their mounts and themselves that they are on a journey.*

Medium Shot—The Four Men: Pablo, Emiliano, Eufemio, and Fernando

FERNANDO *squats in the sand beside the river, picks up a stick and idly draws what might be a half-imagined map in the sand.*

PABLO: He's not a tall man, has a brown beard, soft voice . . . and his hands—

EUFEMIO *(breaking in)*: Doesn't sound like a fighter.

32

PABLO: Well no . . . he's quiet—(EMILIANO *seems abstracted*)

FERNANDO: He's firm and he's brave! —I know he's brave!]

PABLO: We spoke of you, Emiliano.

FERNANDO: He wants a message from you. . . . *(*EMILIANO *does not answer)* One strong push from the north or south and Díaz will drop like an old bull with a sword under his shoulder . . . the time has come!

> EMILIANO *has raised his* HORSE'S *front foot and is pulling off a loose shoe.* EMILIANO SPEAKS *soothingly to the* HORSE.

EMILIANO: Steady, Blanco . . . steady. . . .

EUFEMIO: I don't understand it. How can this Madero stay in the United States? Why don't they lock him up?

FERNANDO: Up there they protect political refugees—

EUFEMIO: Why?

PABLO *(groping for an explanation)*: Well—up there they are a democracy.

EMILIANO: We're a democracy, too, and look what's happened.

PABLO *(earnestly)*: Yes, I know, but up there it—it's different—

FERNANDO *(cutting him very short)*: I will explain it. There the Government governs, but with the consent of the people. The people have a voice.

PABLO: That's right.

FERNANDO *(continuing)*: They have a President, too, but he governs with the consent of the people. Here we have a President, but no consent. Who asked us if we wanted Díaz for thirty-four years?

EUFEMIO: Nobody ever asked me nothing.

> *Suddenly* EMILIANO *turns around from his* HORSE *and looks sharply at* FERNANDO.

EMILIANO: And you—how are *you* in this?

PABLO: Madero sent him with me.

FERNANDO *(to* EMILIANO—*very tough)*: He wants a message from you. I am waiting to hear what to tell him.

EMILIANO (*equally tough*): He wants a leader here. It's not me.

He mounts his HORSE. PABLO *looks at him, shocked.*

FERNANDO: You don't believe in him?

EMILIANO: Yes.

FERNANDO: So?

EMILIANO: Tell him to get another man.

FERNANDO: As you wish.

EMILIANO: I have private affairs. Besides, I don't want to be the conscience of the world. I don't want to be the conscience of anybody.

They glare at each other murderously.

FERNANDO (*tight-lipped*): As you wish.

EMILIANO *turns his* HORSE *and starts across the ford.*

EUFEMIO *splashes into the river, comes abreast of* EMILIANO, *grabs his bridle.*

[*Emiliano and Eufemio*

EUFEMIO (*with great violence*): Why do you want her? Emiliano, I took a very good look—by daylight! Not only isn't she pretty, she's stringy! There's nothing on her! Take a good close look. Why I know twins over in Cuautla, both of them ten times as good and they aren't pretty either. And with money, too! And you can have either one! Or both!

EMILIANO *doesn't answer.* EUFEMIO *releases the* HORSE—EMILIANO *crosses the stream.*]

Dissolve to:
Long Shot—Piece of the Road Ahead

Two mounted RURALES, *leading a* PRISONER.

Medium Shot—Group

There is a noose about the PRISONER's *neck, the other end tied to the saddle horn of one of the* RURALES. *The* PRISONER *is the* OLD INDIAN *who was in the boundary-marking scene,* MEMBER *also of the* DELE-GATION *who called on* DÍAZ. *He has no hat now and is dressed in the ragged white field clothes characteristic of the district. His hands are tied behind him. His face is parched with dirt and sun. There are whip marks on his face. About twenty feet behind him trudges* HIS WIFE, *carrying a big bundle.*

Wider Angle

as EMILIANO, EUFEMIO, *and* PABLO *ride up alongside, pass the* WOMAN *and ride even with the* PRISONER. *They pull their* HORSES *down to a walk.*

EMILIANO: Why, it's Innocente! What's the matter?

Close Shot—Emiliano and the Prisoner

INNOCENTE *looks up. His mouth is dry; he licks his lips, attempts to speak, and then looks down at the road. Suddenly the rope around his neck is jerked.*

FIRST RURALE'S VOICE: Get away from the prisoner!

EMILIANO *(ignoring* RURALE*)*: Innocente, what are they taking you in for?

INNOCENTE *is silent.*

EMILIANO: Innocente?

INNOCENTE *doesn't even look up.*

Wider Angle

as PABLO *and* EUFEMIO *ride up beside* EMILIANO.

PABLO: He can't talk, Emiliano. He's thirsty.

EUFEMIO *reaches for the gourd of water which he carries.*

Another Angle—Including Mounted Rurales

EMILIANO *rides up alongside the* RURALES.

EMILIANO: What did he do?

FIRST RURALE: They're all crazy. They're the craziest people I ever saw.

EMILIANO *(persistently)*: But what did he do?
SECOND RURALE: Who knows. . . . They're always doing something.
EMILIANO: What are you going to do with him?
The RURALES *look at him as if to say:* "How dumb can you get!"
EMILIANO: Let him go.
They look back at the PRISONER.

The Prisoner

EUFEMIO *rides in beside him, holds the water gourd to his mouth, trying to give him a drink.*

Full Shot—Group

Without explanation, or a word, the RURALE *jerks the* OLD MAN *off his feet and the water gourd flies from* EUFEMIO's *hand and breaks on the road. The* OLD MAN *is flat, face downward on the road.*

Another Angle—Favoring Emiliano

He whips out his machete; the RURALE *ducks and whirls his* HORSE *to escape. The* SECOND RURALE *follows him.*

The Prisoner

He has partially risen to his feet; now, since he is tied to the saddle of the fleeing RURALE, *he is again thrown flat, and is dragged along the road.*

Exterior, Road—Moving Shot

as EMILIANO *pursues the fleeing* RURALES. *He closes the distance between them, and slashes at the rope which ties the* PRISONER.

Close Shot—Prisoner

As the rope is cut, the PRISONER *is released, and rolls clear.*

The Two Rurales

> *flee into the field of cane alongside the road, and disappear from view.*

Emiliano

> *He whirls around, starts back to* GROUP *around the* PRISONER.

Exterior, Road—Group Around Innocente's Body

> INNOCENTE'S WIFE *is beside him . . . turning him over. He is dead. The* PEOPLE *of the fields appear from the cane. They surround the body.* EMILIANO *rides in, dismounts.* FERNANDO *rides in to the* GROUP.

WIFE *(to the body)*: I told you and I warned you. You couldn't get it through your head. The land isn't ours any more. Even after they killed Plutarco, you went in at night to plant the field.

Close Shot—Emiliano and Fernando

FERNANDO: You should have cut the rope, without talking.

EMILIANO: It was my fault. I should have cut the rope and then talked.

Wider Angle—Group

WIFE *(accusingly to the corpse)*: You're headstrong, that's what you are. You always have been. You're stubborn.

> EUFEMIO *and* PABLO *come near to* EMILIANO. *Other* INDIANS, *among them* LAZARO, *have appeared from nowhere.*

EMILIANO *(to* EUFEMIO *and* PABLO): He's dead.

WIFE *(still to the corpse)*: You crawled through the fence at night to plant the corn.

AN INDIAN: My father does the same thing. . . .

WIFE *(still scolding the corpse)*: Stubborn—that's what you are. . . .

LAZARO (*defending the body gently*): No . . . not stubborn . . . the field is like a wife . . . live with it all your life, it's hard to learn that she isn't yours. (*gesturing toward* EMILIANO) *He* understands.

WIFE (*turns to* EMILIANO, *apologetically*): I'm sorry we caused you trouble. . . .

ANOTHER INDIAN: Now they'll be after you. . . .

LAZARO: You can hide in my house. . . .

ANOTHER INDIAN: I'll take care of your horse. . . .

> EMILIANO *removes his hat, leans down toward the body.*

EMILIANO: I'm sorry, Innocente. . . .

> *He turns, quickly mounts his* HORSE, *and rides off in fury.*

Fernando and Pablo stand looking after him. Fernando smiles.

Dissolve to:
Interior, Small Half-Warehouse, Half-Office

> *The business place of* SEÑOR ESPEJO, *which is one section of the* ESPEJO *home. Packages and bales of soaps, candles and basic hardware which* ESPEJO *imports and sells.* SEÑOR ESPEJO *sits behind his desk,* EMILIANO *stands before it.*

EMILIANO: Don Nacio is my patron. He has assured me that I will be a man of substance. On this basis I presume to sue for your daughter's hand.

> SEÑOR ESPEJO *rises, and as he speaks he casually walks to the door which separates the living quarters from the business quarters of his establishment and opens it a few inches. The opened door discloses for the audience (but not for* EMILIANO) *the figures of* JOSEFA, *her* MOTHER, *and her* AUNT, *sitting primly, each with her embroidery frame. They lean forward, listening, but pretending not to.*

SEÑOR ESPEJO *to* EMILIANO (*as he is opening the door*): My friend, do not think I am insensible of the honor you

39

do me in offering to take my daughter off my hands. But I do not need to give the problem a great deal of thought before I answer with a permanent and unchanging NO! The answer is no. . . .

EMILIANO: What's the matter with me?

SEÑOR ESPEJO *(returning to his desk, seating himself):* There is a proverb: "Though we are all made of the same clay, a jug is not a vase."

EMILIANO: What's the matter with me?

SEÑOR ESPEJO: I hoped you would not ask that again, but since you have, allow me to say that you are a rancher without land, a gentleman without money, a man of substance without substance!

He looks toward the door to the living quarters.

Interior, Living Quarters

The embroidering has stopped. The WOMEN *are listening.* JOSEFA *leans forward, intently listening.*

Espejo and Emiliano

SEÑOR ESPEJO *is* SPEAKING *now especially for his* WOMEN.

SEÑOR ESPEJO: A fighter, a drinker, a brawler; these things you are. I have nothing against you personally. I can see where in some quarters you might be considered desirable. But my daughter! I have no intention whatsoever of one day finding her squatting on the bare earth, patting tortillas like a common Indian.

There is silence for a moment. Then EMILIANO *strikes the desk with his hand. The papers jump out of their pigeonholes.* SEÑOR ESPEJO *leaps back with fear. A nineteenth-century Shepherdess of cheap plaster falls and crashes.*

EMILIANO: Don't be afraid, little man. *(*EMILIANO *crosses to the door of the living quarters)*

SEÑOR ESPEJO: What are you doing?

EMILIANO: Find her a merchant—a musty, moth-eaten man like yourself.

He has said this in the direction of the door. Now he opens it wide, revealing the WOMEN *listening. The* OLDER WOMEN *are terribly frightened.* JOSEFA *is rather pleased, smiling. . . .*

EMILIANO: Let her be queen of the warehouses and mistress of the receipt books!

He turns toward the front door and steps through into the street. . . .

Exterior, Espejo's Office

As EMILIANO *exits, he is pinned down by both arms. Many* RURALES *hold him. They are taking no chances with* EMILIANO. *Among the large force of* MEN *are the* TWO RURALES *whom* EMILIANO *met on the road with the* PRISONER. *Expertly the* MEN *begin to bind* EMILIANO's *arms behind him.*

Full Shot—Village Square

At this moment a little crowd of PEOPLE *come slowly across the square, carrying a body on a rude litter made of two poles and a serape. They see that* EMILIANO *is being arrested and know it is because of what he tried to do for them.*

Exterior, Square

The RURALES *lead* EMILIANO *away. The* PEOPLE *watch. Then they all turn and look toward* ESPEJO's *store.*

Close Shot—Señor Espejo standing in his doorway. He becomes aware of the Indians. He turns, enters his store, closes the door.

The Street

About a dozen RURALES *now surround* EMILIANO, *whose hands are tied behind him.* FEATURE *this tying.*

Pablo and Eufemio watching—then they ride off.

Group Shot of people watching. They know what is intended for Emiliano. Beginning of the summoning of the People.

Emiliano and Rurales

> Twelve RURALES, *six on either side of* EMILIANO. *His hands are tied behind him; he is on foot, and he is led by the neck by a rope which the* OFFICER *riding ahead of him holds.*

Close Shot—Emiliano

> *as his eyes quickly search the* CROWD. *There is a change of expression as he sees—*

Eufemio, Pablo, and Fernando

> *among the* CROWD. *They stare back at* EMILIANO.

Close Shot—Emiliano

> *He looks away from* EUFEMIO, PABLO, *and* FERNANDO, *stares straight ahead.*

Full Shot—Procession

> *as it starts down the street,* EMILIANO *walking between the* TWO COLUMNS OF RURALES.

Quick Dissolve to:
Exterior, Road Past the Original Field

> *The* PROCESSION *on the move. In the distance, ahead of the* PROCESSION, *a few* COUNTRY PEOPLE *are casually walking along.*

Exterior, Cane Field

> *A* GROUP OF COUNTRY PEOPLE *moving secretly through the cane.*

Exterior, Road—Near a Corner

The PROCESSION *rounds a corner and ahead of them are trudging a large* GROUP OF COUNTRY PEOPLE.

Close Shot—Captain of Rurales

He sees the COUNTRY PEOPLE; *then he turns and looks back.*

What He Sees

GROUP OF COUNTRY PEOPLE *following, very casually.*

Clòse Shot—Captain, frowning.

Dissolve to:
Road Through Hilly Country

The PROCESSION *moves along.* SHOOTING ACROSS THE COLUMN *we see a mass of* PEOPLE *moving down a hill.*

Close Shot—Rurales, apprehensive.

Close Shot—Captain, very apprehensive.

Full Shot—Procession

now surrounded on all sides by PEOPLE *pressing on them. Movement is becoming very difficult. The* COUNTRY PEOPLE *look straight ahead as they trudge along.*

Close-up—Emiliano, in midst of Procession.

The Procession

We are SHOOTING DOWN *on them. As they move along* CAMERA RISES, *and we see ahead a line of* MOUNTED AND ARMED MEN *blocking the road.*

Medium, Shot—Mounted Men

EUFEMIO, PABLO, *and* FERNANDO *prominent among them.* EUFEMIO *holds the reins of* EMILIANO'S WHITE HORSE.

44

Close Shot—Captain

He looks at the MOUNTED MEN, *then turns in the saddle and looks back at* EMILIANO.

Close Shot—Emiliano

He stares back, *without expression.*

The Procession

The CAPTAIN *holds up his hand and the* PROCESSION *stops a few feet from the* MOUNTED MEN. EMILIANO *looks up a little sardonically. The* CAPTAIN *rises in his stirrups, and* YELLS *to the* MOUNTED MEN:

CAPTAIN: Clear the way!

No movement. No answer.

Close Shot—Captain

CAPTAIN (*a little hysterically*): This man is a criminal! You are making yourselves liable for his crime!

Group Shot—Mounted Men

No movement at all. No answer. They stare back impassively.

Close Shot—Captain

He looks toward the MOUNTED MEN, *then looks around at the* COUNTRY PEOPLE, *who surround the* COLUMN.

CAPTAIN: What are you trying to do?

Medium Shot—Group of Indians

LAZARO: We are here, my Captain, with your permission, to see that the prisoner does not try to escape. For if he did try, you would be forced to shoot him in the back. Is it not so, my Captain?

Captain—and Column, Including Emiliano

After a pause, the CAPTAIN CRIES:

CAPTAIN: You're defying the law!

45

LAZARO: No, helping the law, with your permission—Guarding the prisoner!

OTHERS CHIME IN. *There is another pause. Then the* CAPTAIN *turns his* HORSE, *goes back a few paces to* EMILIANO, *takes out a knife and cuts the ropes which bind his hands.* EMILIANO *looks up at him without expression.*

Full Shot

as EMILIANO *walks from the midst of the* COLUMNS *to the* GROUP OF MOUNTED MEN, *takes the reins of his* HORSE *from* EUFEMIO.

Group Shot—Mounted Men and Emiliano

He stands beside his HORSE, *puts his hand between the cinch and the belly.*

EMILIANO *(to the* HORSE*)*: Blanco! The cinch is too loose!

He tightens the cinch and mounts. PABLO *hands him his hat.*

Group Shot—Captain and Rurales

The CAPTAIN *is livid at this defiance.*

Group Shot—Country People

Looking toward EMILIANO *in a new way. Somehow through this incident he has become the leader of these* PEOPLE.

Emiliano, Eufemio, Pablo, Fernando, and the Mounted Men

EMILIANO *(to* EUFEMIO, *with wonder—looking off toward the* PEOPLE*)*: How did they all get here?

EUFEMIO *(with a smile and a shrug)*: Who knows . . . ? Let's go. . . .

FERNANDO: Zapata!—the wire—

EMILIANO: What do you mean?

FERNANDO: The telegraph wire. Cut it before he uses it—

Wider Angle

as EUFEMIO *rides to the lowest place in the telegraph wire loop and reaches up with his machete.*

Close Shot—Captain as he sees what Eufemio is about to do.

CAPTAIN: Don't touch that! This is rebellion!

Eufemio

standing high in his stirrups, machete raised. He pauses, looks at EMILIANO.

Close Shot—Emiliano

He looks back at EUFEMIO.

EMILIANO: Cut it.

Eufemio

He brings his machete down on the wire. The wires spring apart.

Emiliano and Mounted Men

As EUFEMIO *rides back to them. They whirl, ride away.*

Full Shot—Road

The COUNTRY PEOPLE *suddenly and silently melt away. The twelve* RURALES *are on a deserted road. They look at each other . . . and then around at the deserted country.*

                                                        Fade out

[*Fade in*
A Pavilion in a Garden of a Hacienda—Evening

This is the home of DON NACIO. *Lanterns provide illumination. Flowers, shrubs,* SINGING *birds in gilt cages.* STRINGS PLAYING *a waltz,* SOFTLY. *On a tiled roof,*

47

directly above the ORCHESTRA, *concealed by the leaves of a banana tree,* TWO LITTLE INDIAN BOYS *watch.*

Full Shot—Dinner Table

INDIANS, *dressed in the white clothes of the period, and under the direction of a French* MAJOR-DOMO, *serve the* GUESTS. *This is a dinner party given by* DON NACIO *for two of his neighbor* hacendados. *One of them,* GENERAL FUENTES, *wears the full-dress uniform of a Mexican general, with decorations that include the Iron Cross. The other man is* DON GARCÍA. *Their* WIVES *are rather dumpy, food stultified, and overdressed. They sit like bug-eating plants. At the opposite end of the table from* DON NACIO *is a* WOMAN *who is ravishingly beautiful.* DON NACIO, *it will appear, is somewhat drunk.*

Medium Shot—Group at Table

DON NACIO *(speaking very earnestly, and with difficulty)*: Gentlemen, my family has been here three hundred years. I know the facts. These fields *do* belong to the Indian villages since before the Conquest!

DON GARCÍA: I paid for the land! I put the money in the hands of one who sits next to President Díaz himself!

GENERAL FUENTES: I remember very well a similar incident.

DON NACIO *(earnestly)*: Give the land back. You don't need it. You have so much. . . .

DON GARCÍA: Don Nacio, you're drunk . . . or indisposed.

DON NACIO: I'm drunk—with wine and with worry. We're all in danger. If we don't give a little—we'll lose it all. . . . *(repeating with new conviction)* The village people have been on that land for a thousand years. They own it.

DON GARCÍA: I paid for it! *I* own it!

DON NACIO *(suddenly turning to one of the waiters—* MANUEL*)*: Isn't that right, Manuel? A thousand years?

MANUEL: Yes, Don Nacio.

DON NACIO: Manuel is from Anencuilco. . . . You don't know these Indians—they're fierce people.

MANUEL: Yes, Don Nacio. . . .

DON NACIO: They will fight for their fields.

GENERAL FUENTES: With what? With what will they fight? As a military man, I'm curious. . . .

DON GARCÍA *(suddenly exploding with rage)*: Don't you think *I'll* fight? Don't you?

His WIFE *calms him. She gives him a pill. He takes it.*

GENERAL FUENTES: It seems ridiculous to ruin this beautiful dinner with politics. . . . *(referring to* DON NACIO's LADY) Don Nacio, why do you raise sugar when you have such sweets already at your table. . . .

DON GARCÍA: Sugar! You know I am not an absentee farmer. I am a scientist. I know land. And this land was made for sugar . . . made by God himself. I say so in all reverence: for sugar. . . . Not corn!

DON NACIO: But they eat corn.

DON GARCÍA *(to his* WIFE, *who is trying to get his attention)*: What?

GARCÍA's WIFE: The cream, dear.

DON GARCÍA: What?

GARCÍA's WIFE: The cream . . . only the cream, if you please.

DON GARCÍA *(LOUDLY)*: Yes, of course, the cream . . . *(does not pass it)* We will transform this land from a corn-ridden desert to a paradise. These animals can't be expected to understand the science of agriculture. Don't misconstrue me. The Indian is my neighbor. I *like* the Indians, and they *love me. (to his* WIFE) Don't they?

GARCÍA's WIFE *(chewing)*: They adore you.

DON NACIO: They eat corn!

DON GARCÍA: Sugar cane. The money from sugar will reach everywhere. I foresee a land of happy families. You'll see the whole population rising.

DON NACIO *(apparently he has given up)*: I think they've risen.

Full Shot—Pavilion

From out of the undergrowth and the beautifully land-scaped garden, WHITE FIGURES *silently arising all around the pavilion on which the dinner is being served. They are expressionless, silent, stolid. They hold machetes. Among them stands* EMILIANO. *The* GUESTS *look around.*

DON GARCÍA: What is it? Who are they?

DON NACIO: Some of your neighbors. They love you.

PABLO *comes forward, dressed in white field clothes, holding his hat over his breast humbly. . . .*

Medium Shot—at Table

PABLO *(to* DON NACIO*)*: Emiliano Zapata wants to know, have you reached a conclusion. . . . He can't wait longer.

DON GARCÍA *and* GENERAL FUENTES *look at* DON NACIO *for an explanation.*

DON NACIO *(turning to other* MEN*)*: Emiliano Zapata came to me this morning. He asked my help in restoring the village lands, before the country burns up with fighting. The most I could offer him was to call you gentlemen together and beg you to stop this tragedy.

GENERAL FUENTES: The Army will stop this tragedy! They're on the way.

DON NACIO *(again trying desperately to make them understand)*: He came this afternoon—oh, I told you that. He wanted help, he wanted money, he wanted food, he wanted some weapons from my little armory. Why am I drunk? I couldn't give him help. I knew he was right, but I didn't have the courage to help him.

PABLO: Excuse me, sir, but—

EMILIANO'S VOICE *(silencing him)*: Pablo—

DON NACIO *(to* EMILIANO*)*: The Army. Did you hear, Emiliano? I didn't send for them.

Close Shot—Emiliano

EMILIANO: Good-by, Don Nacio.

He turns, walks away.

Full Shot—Dinner Table

GENERAL FUENTES *takes a pistol from his holster and points from the waist at* EMILIANO's *back.* DON NACIO *grabs his wrist.* MANUEL, *the Indian servant, sees this; he removes his coat, puts it on a chair and follows* EMILIANO.

GENERAL FUENTES (*to* DON NACIO): By saving him you may have killed a thousand men. You may have killed yourself.

DON NACIO *goes to the edge of the platform, stands there, looking off into the darkness.*

Close Shot—Don García

DON GARCÍA (*suddenly horror-stricken*): If there's fighting, who'll harvest the sugar cane??!!

Full Shot—Group—Favoring Don Nacio

Over scene comes the SOUND *of* TWO MEASURED THUMPS *and a* SMALL CRASH *of shattering wood. The* GUESTS *react in alarm. A smile appears on* DON NACIO's *face, rueful and proud.*

DON NACIO: If you don't give a little, they'll take it all.

Now there is a GREAT CRASH, *and splintering of wood.*

DON GARCÍA (*alarmed*): What's that?

DON NACIO: My armory. *Now* they have weapons.

They all stare at one another. As DON NACIO *starts to pour himself a drink—*

Dissolve to:
Exterior, a Road—a Brilliant Moonlit Night

A platoon of mounted FEDERAL SOLDIERS *on the march. We* HEAR *a series of* SHORT COYOTE BARKS. *The road at one point is flanked by trees, whose branches overhang and meet. As they enter the arch of branches—*

Close Shot—Man Behind Rock—Side of Road

He raises his head, cups his hand around his mouth and gives a FULL COYOTE HOWL.

Close Shot—Two Officers, at Head of Procession

ONE OFFICER *(to the* OTHER*)*: What was that?

OTHER OFFICER: Coyote.

The FIRST OFFICER *nods, trying to dismiss his fears. But he looks around apprehensively.*

Head-on Shot—Procession

at it enters the arch of trees. The COYOTE HOWL ECHOES *through the valley. At this signal,* FIGURES *drop from the branches onto the mounted* FEDERALS. *Instantly the orderly* COLUMN *has become a plunging, struggling, tangling mass of* MEN *and* HORSES.

Dissolve to:
Close Shot—Emiliano on Horseback looking off into the trees.

Wider Angle

Out from under the trees appears a PROCESSION OF IN- DIANS, *leading the* HORSES *of the troops loaded with the equipment, clothing, arms, even the shoes of the now extinct soldiers. Some* INDIANS *with armloads of rifles.* EUFEMIO *is directing the* MEN. *He rides over to* EMILIANO.

Two Shot—Emiliano and Eufemio

EUFEMIO: Wait till you see some of the horses!

EMILIANO: How about bullets?

EUFEMIO: No pack animals, but wonderful horses! What horses!

Wider Angle

A circle of ZAPATISTAS, *all carrying various pieces of captured equipment, surround* EMILIANO. *Some hold their prizes in the air.*

EMILIANO: But bullets—we need ammunition—what good are horses? How can we fight without bullets and ammunition?

52

Suddenly he spins his horse around with a violent angry gesture and rides away. The OTHERS *follow.*]

Dissolve to:
A Deep Gulch, as Seen from a Spot High Above

A railroad track runs through the gulch. A train of boxcars, with TROOPS *on top, is entering the gulch.*

Medium Shot—a Little Gasoline Handcar, its whole front loaded with dynamite, is racing along the railroad track.

Long Shot—Shooting from Above the Gulch

Now we see that the handcar is speeding toward *the oncoming train. It hits. There is a* TREMENDOUS EX-PLOSION.

Full Shot

From all sides of the gulch come WHITE-CLAD FIG-URES; *they swarm over the train like bees.*

Moving Shot—at Train

Along the string of boxcars come EMILIANO, *and* PABLO, *preceded by* MEN *who are breaking open the car doors. They stop at a door. The* MEN *who have opened it look out.*

EMILIANO: What is it?

A ZAPATISTA: Canned beef.

The GROUP *moves on to the next car, pause.*

EMILIANO: What is it?

A ZAPATISTA: Uniforms and blankets.

The GROUP *moves on to the next car, pause.*

EMILIANO: What is it?

ZAPATISTA: A piano . . . some furniture—

There is a SUDDEN SHOUT *from up ahead.* EMILIANO *and his entourage run forward, up to a boxcar that has a door thrown open.* EUFEMIO *is standing at the door of a boxcar which has been fixed up as a kind*

53

of traveling ladies' apartment. Inside there are THREE
GIRLS, *frightened to death, and an old tough-looking*
WOMAN, *probably a procurer of some kind, who stares
defiantly at the* MEN. EMILIANO *looks at them for a
moment. Then there is* ANOTHER SHOUT *from up ahead.*
EMILIANO *moves up to another car.*

EMILIANO: Ammunition?

A ZAPATISTA *comes to the door of the boxcar.*

ZAPATISTA: No . . . but powder and dynamite.

EMILIANO: How much?

ZAPATISTA: Half a car. . . .

EMILIANO: No ammunition?

ZAPATISTA: No. . . .

EMILIANO *(after a pause)*: We won't wait any longer!
We'll use what we have.

Dissolve to:
**The Tower of the Citadel in a Garrison Town—the Hour
Before Dawn**

*In the foreground a machine gun, pointing at the plaza.
We see an empty plaza with a small bandstand in the
middle.* MACHINE GUNNERS *are anxiously looking over
the parapet. An* OFFICER *(*CAPTAIN*) approaches. The
scene that follows should be shot entirely from the
viewpoint of these* MEN.

CAPTAIN: Anything moving?

FIRST SOLDIER: A few women.

SECOND SOLDIER: I liked it better when they were shooting.

CAPTAIN: Maybe Zapata ran out of ammunition.

SECOND SOLDIER: I wouldn't depend on that.

FIRST SOLDIER: I think they've gone away. . . . Look
there, sir, some market women. If there's a market, they
must have gone away.

SECOND SOLDIER: With these Indians I don't trust the
women any more than the men. . . .

CAPTAIN: But there hasn't been a sign of them since yesterday noon. I'm going to send out some scouts. *(looks over the parapet and* CALLS *down to the* WOMEN*)* What are you doing down there?

The Gate—Shooting Down from the Tower

The WOMEN *stop in front of the gate and look up. (Among the* WOMEN *is the* SOLDADERA.*)*
CAPTAIN: What are you doing down there?
SOLDADERA: Going to market, sir.
CAPTAIN: Get away from the gate. . . .
SOLDADERA: Would you like to buy some eggs, sir?
CAPTAIN: Get away from the gate!

Medium Shot—Old Women at Gate

The SOLDADERA *speaks rapidly in the Indian language to the other* WOMEN. *They pile their baskets in a cluster against the gate.*
CAPTAIN'S VOICE: Get away from the gate or we'll shoot you!
The SOLDADERA *gives a short sharp order and the* WOMEN *scuttle away like chickens in all directions.*

Exterior, Tower of the Citadel

The CAPTAIN *turns to* ONE OF HIS MEN.
CAPTAIN: Go down and get those baskets—quick!
The MAN *exits quickly.*

Street in Town

A wild-looking WOMAN *comes out of a side street, carrying a torch. The* SOUND *of a* MACHINE GUN *comes over. The* WOMAN *falls. Immediately she pulls herself up, starts to crawl, still carrying the torch. With a final effort she reaches her goal—a powder train which has been laid in the plaza. She sets the torch to the powder train. Another* BURST OF MACHINE-GUN FIRE *hits her, kills her.*

Exterior, Plaza

*The powder train runs quickly across the plaza, toward
the* CAMERA. *There is a huge* EXPLOSION *right in the
face of the* CAMERA.

Series of Quick Shots

of MEN *pouring out of doors, racing around street cor-
ners.*

Full Shot—Plaza

*Through the smoke and debris we see a charge of
masses of* SHOUTING MEN. *Some on foot, some on
horseback. At the height of the charge—*

Dissolve to:
The Tower of the Citadel—Day

The machine gun is gone. Bodies of the MACHINE GUN-
NERS *and of* ZAPATISTAS *lying about. The* CAMERA
MOVES OVER *to the parapet,* SHOOTS DOWN *on the
plaza. Now it is full of* ZAPATISTA TROOPS, *camped on
their equipment.*

Full Shot—Plaza

The MEN *who won the victory are lying about on their
serapes, resting, eating, and generally celebrating.*
WOMEN *and* CHILDREN *are clustered around them.*

The Bandstand

PEOPLE *crowd around the bandstand, looking up at:*

Emiliano seated at a carved state table.

*The table is littered with gifts: fruits, piles of flowers,
chickens, a small trussed pig.* EMILIANO *sits in a state
chair at one end of the table, holding court, adminis-
tering justice, giving rewards. [Behind him an* OLD
INDIAN WOMAN *is cooking tortillas and passing them
to the young and lovely* JUANA *(a girl we have not seen*

before), who makes the tacos as she knows EMILIANO
*likes them and hands them to him, one at a time, as
the scene progresses.* EUFEMIO *and* PABLO *are nearby.*

Angle at the Table

A WOMAN *comes up with a bouquet of flowers.*
WOMAN: A present for you, my chief.
EMILIANO *(taking them):* Thank you.
He puts them on the table. The WOMAN *moves away.*
JUANA *hands him a glass of pulque. Her warm eyes
tell us how much this man means to her.*

Another Angle at the Table

Another WOMAN *approaches, looks intently at* EMILI-
ANO.
EMILIANO: Yes?
WOMAN *(peering into his face as though to memorize
it):* I want to see you close up.
She steps aside as a tough, grizzly GUERRILLA FIGHTER
comes up, pulling a reluctant LITTLE BOY *by the arm.*]

Three Shot—Emiliano, Guerrilla Fighter (Eduardo), and Little Boy

EDUARDO: Emiliano, remember that machine gun that
flanked us from the hill. . . .
EMILIANO: Yes?
EDUARDO *(almost incredulously):* This boy and his
brother crept out in the dark. They lassoed that gun and
pulled it right out of the gunner's hands. Look at the
size of him!
EMILIANO *(to* BOY): Did you do that?
The LITTLE BOY *drops his head.*
EDUARDO: Sure he did *(he* SHOUTS) Bring the machine
gun!
EMILIANO: Leave the gun. . . . *(to the* BOY) Did you do
that?
LITTLE BOY *(forcing the words out):* Yes, my chief.

EMILIANO: Where's your brother?

EDUARDO: He was killed. . . .

EMILIANO: You should have a reward. . . . *(pointing)* Want that pig?

The LITTLE BOY *looks at the pig, then slowly his eyes move around and he looks past* EMILIANO. EMILIANO *follows his gaze, and sees:*

His Own Horse held by a Soldier.

Back to Scene

EMILIANO: Not my horse? *(*LITTLE BOY *frowns. It's a problem. Then he nods)* That's a good horse.

LITTLE BOY WHISPERS *something.* EDUARDO *bends over then straightens up and says:*

EDUARDO: He says that's why he wants it.

EMILIANO *(to the* BOY*)*: Take it!

The LITTLE BOY *turns and scuttles away.* EMILIANO *rises, stands looking down into the plaza, munching on a tortilla which* JUANA *hands him.*

Exterior, Plaza—near Bandstand

The LITTLE BOY *rushes in to* EMILIANO'S HORSE, *attempts to take the reins from the* SOLDIER. *The* SOLDIER *looks up at* EMILIANO.

Angle at Bandstand—Emiliano

looking down at the GROUP. *He nods to the* SOLDIER.

Group at Horse

The SOLDIER *helps the* LITTLE BOY *into the saddle. He turns, smiles up at* EMILIANO, *rides out of the square.*

Close Shot—Emiliano, back to Camera, looking off at the disappearing Horse. He turns, stops suddenly.

Wider Angle

EMILIANO *is face to face with* SEÑOR ESPEJO, *dressed in his best. Standing immediately behind him is a tough* ZAPATISTA *with a bandaged head. This is* LA-ZARO, *who has now become a toughened guerrilla fighter.*

EMILIANO *(with a certain anticipated pleasure)*: What did he *do?*

LAZARO: I don't know.

SEÑOR ESPEJO: Don Emiliano, my friend, I wish to present representatives of our great liberator, Francisco Madero.

EMILIANO: What!!!???

Full Shot—Group on Bandstand

SEÑOR ESPEJO: Gentlemen—here he is—

He turns, looks toward THREE OFFICERS *in the uniform of the North.* FERNANDO *is with them.*

SEÑOR ESPEJO:—Don Emiliano Zapata, one of my oldest acquaintances.

FERNANDO *(with irony)*: We know each other. My congratulations, General Zapata.

EUFEMIO, *who has come up beside* EMILIANO, *reaches across him to make a taco, looks up to* EMILIANO.

EMILIANO: General?

FERNANDO *puts a sealed document on the table.* EU-FEMIO *bends over. Some chili from his taco falls on the paper.* EMILIANO *picks it up and wipes it on his sleeve.*

EMILIANO: Pablo. . . . *(*PABLO *comes up)* Read it.

Two Shot—Emiliano and Pablo

PABLO *opens paper and reads it to himself. Looks at* ZAPATA.

EMILIANO: Well, read it.

PABLO *(reads)*: "To Emiliano Zapata. I, Francisco Madero, acting on the authority given me by the forces of triumphant liberation, create you General of the Armies of the South. . . . May the day soon come when I embrace you in triumph! Long live Mexico!" *(impressed)* And he signed it with his own hand.

EMILIANO *snatches the paper and inspects it. He looks up with childlike pleasure....*

Group Shot

EUFEMIO *(to* EMILIANO*)*: Now you'll have to wear those things a general wears.

He pulls a general's cap ornament out of his pocket and throws it on the table. EMILIANO *picks it up.*

SEÑOR ESPEJO *(coming forward)*: I and my family will be very happy if you will honor us with—

EMILIANO *(paying no attention to him—to* EUFEMIO, *indicating the cap ornament)*: Where did you get it?

EUFEMIO: Off a general....

SEÑOR ESPEJO *(trying again)*: I and my family—

AN INDIAN WOMAN *(pushing* ESPEJO *aside)*: A present, my general....

She thrusts a large dirty bouquet of live trussed chickens into his hands.... EMILIANO *holds in one hand the chickens, the other, the general's ornaments.*

Dissolve to:
[*The Town Square—Night*

Little fires with the "JUANS" *(cf. our GIs) squatting around, fed by their* WOMEN *who cook at the little fires.* PANORAMIC SHOT *to a* MAN *and a* WOMAN *by a little fire and it is* EMILIANO. *He has a serape around his shoulders, like all the other* INDIANS. *To the right and slightly behind him is a pretty* INDIAN GIRL *cooking the tortillas and wrapping each one around bits of meat.*

Close Shot—Emiliano and Juana

ZAPATA, *thinking deeply while he eats. As he finishes one taco, he reaches out his hand, without looking at the* GIRL. *She puts a cup of pulque in his hand, he swallows it, hands it back, still without looking at her.*

She puts another taco in his hand. He never looks at her.

JUANA: Eat.

EMILIANO: No.

JUANA: Had enough?

EMILIANO: Yes.

JUANA *puts the chili and meat in her basket and covers it with a cloth. Then she comes and sits on the ground close to him and embraces his leg in a gesture of the nakedest kind of love. She looks up at him, her eyes full of desire. He looks at her. It is very hard now to say what he has to say, but he does.*

EMILIANO: You will have to go now, Juana. I don't need you any more.

She doesn't move. He touches her with affection.

EMILIANO: I will give you a cornfield. You will never go hungry.

Meekly JUANA *arranges her rebozo over her face in a very modest way, picks up her basket of food, and moves off.*

Juana—Moving Shot

She walks among the fires. She looks at various GROUPS OF SOLDIERS *being fed by* WOMEN *and at length comes to a* VERY YOUNG SOLDIER, *sitting on the ground. She looks at him a moment, and he looks back at her, expressionless. Then without a word she squats down, fans up her little charcoal fire, and begins to pat out a tortilla. He looks at her. He leans back, smiles.*

Dissolve to:]
Exterior, Espejo Home—Late Afternoon

PABLO *is looking through a barred window into a room where we see* EMILIANO *with* THREE WOMEN. *The* CAMERA *travels along to a second window, where* EUFEMIO *and* FERNANDO *are looking in.*

EUFEMIO (*disapprovingly*): What a waste of time. He should have stolen her if he wanted her.

FERNANDO: This way he gets her father's money, too.

A couple of GIRLS *stroll by, and as he speaks* EUFEMIO *turns to look after them.*

EUFEMIO: But is it worth this?? While he's still after this one, I've loved with all my heart one hundred women I never want to see again. (*he shakes his head in bewilderment*) It escapes me.

Interior, Espejo Home

The stiff parlor of the ESPEJO *home. Small, uncomfortable chairs; heavy framed pictures, religious figures.* EMILIANO *and* JOSEFA *sit in the center of the room. On* JOSEFA's *right, her* MOTHER; *on* EMILIANO's *left,* JOSEFA's *middle-aged* AUNT. *Both are embroidering—in background is seen* SEÑOR ESPEJO. JOSEFA *is dressed in an all-covering dress that comes to the floor.* EMILIANO *is wearing his brilliant charro costume. His hat and carbine on the floor beside him.* EMILIANO *and* JOSEFA *look at each other and then at their flanking* FEMALE GUARDS. EMILIANO *tries to break the silence.*

EMILIANO: Did you think of me . . . ?

The CHAPERONS *stop their work, and straighten up. Their disapproval is clearly conveyed.*

JOSEFA: It is said that a warrior's shield is his sweetheart's heart.

EMILIANO: Uh?

JOSEFA *has spoken in the customary manner of a courtship, i.e., through the traditional "saying."* EMILIANO *for a moment doesn't "get" it.*

JOSEFA (*admiring his gorgeous charro outfit*): We have a proverb: A man well dressed is a man well thought of.

EMILIANO (*now getting it*): A monkey in silk is still a monkey. (JOSEFA *beams approvingly*) But when love—

(he indicates himself)—and beauty—*(indicates* JOSEFA*)* —come in the house, throw out the lamps.

Exterior, House—Fernando and Eufemio

FERNANDO: Listen to that!

EUFEMIO *(spitting)*: Makes me sick! But that! The way these people go about getting married!

> *He swivels his head around to look at a* PASSING GIRL. *She smiles.*

EUFEMIO *(to* FERNANDO*)*: Excuse me.

> *He takes off after the* GIRL.

Interior, Parlor

JOSEFA: Do you believe the saying: An egg unbroke, a horse unrode, a girl unwed?

EMILIANO: I believe that man is fire and woman fuel. *(looks at her closely)* She who is born beautiful is born married. . . .

> JOSEFA *flutters. She leans toward him. Then constrains herself, fans her face and bosom violently. The* WOMEN *unconsciously pick this up and all begin to fan themselves. It is hot and the formal clothes are no help. . . .* EMILIANO *looks around.*

Interior, Parlor—Shooting toward Windows

> *The windows are jammed with* SPECTATORS, *all watching.*

EMILIANO: Get away from those windows—let a little air through.

> *He sees his* WHITE HORSE, *with the* LITTLE BOY *sitting on its back. They are watching the courtship.*

EMILIANO: Get that horse out of here. . . . *(muttering to himself)* Best horse I ever had . . . that's rubbing my nose in it.

> *Again he looks toward the windows, which are abso-*

lutely jammed with SPECTATORS: SOLDIERS, CHILDREN, WOMEN, *all of whom watch without expression.*

Medium Shot—Emiliano, Josefa, Mother, and Aunt

EMILIANO: Josefa, let's go for a walk. There might be a breeze in the park.

Of course this is not allowed until after *the wedding. The* THREE WOMEN *stiffen. The* MOTHER *and* AUNT MURMUR, *incredulously,* "A walk?!" "Alone?" EMILI-ANO *looks from one to the other and realizes he is quite out of step. He looks at* JOSEFA, SIGHS.

EMILIANO: A whipped dog is a wiser dog.

JOSEFA *(coming to his rescue)*: Do you think that three women and a goose make a market? *(she looks at him waiting)*

Slowly he rises and takes a traditional position. The women lean forward. He speaks with measured significance.

EMILIANO: I think that love cannot be bought except with love. *(with faces of the* WOMEN—*very much as if they were kicking in a horse*—*encouraging him. He proceeds)* And he who has a good wife—*(bows, puts his hand over his heart)*—wears heaven in his hat.

It is over. He has proposed. The WOMEN SIGH *with relief, settle back.*

Close Shot—Eufemio—at Window

He disgustedly pulls his hat down over his eyes. Then he looks up quickly as the sound of EXCITED VOICES *comes over. He moves away from the window.*

Interior, Parlor—the Three Women and Emiliano

MOTHER: After love, food. A cup of chocolate?

Over scene we hear the SOUND OF EXCITED VOICES *getting closer.*

EMILIANO: A starved body has a skinny soul.

They all look at him with admiration; they COO *the Mexican equivalent of* "Isn't that sweet."

Another Angle, Shooting toward Window

PABLO *suddenly appears in the window.*
PABLO: Emiliano—
EMILIANO: Go away. *(to* AUNT*)* The pediment of the heart . . . *(with a bow)* . . . is the stomach. . . .
The MAIDEN AUNT *melts,* GIGGLES.
MOTHER: Alicia Candelaria, will you bring chocolate?
PABLO: Emiliano—
EMILIANO: Go away!
PABLO: Emiliano, Díaz has run away; he's left the country!

As if on cue, FIRING BREAKS OUT *in the streets,* HIGH LAUGHTER, CATCALLS, *more* SHOTS. *Everybody is* FIRING *his rifle in the air. All hell breaks loose outside.*

Two Shot—Emiliano and Josefa

His face is suffused with triumph and pleasure. He throws himself at JOSEFA *and takes her in his arms.*
EMILIANO: Josefa, Josefa . . . the fighting is over . . . the fighting is over! *(he's about to kiss her)*
MOTHER'S VOICE: Josefa. *(sharply)* Josefa!
JOSEFA *(to her* MOTHER*)*: Mama! Quiet! *(looking at* EMILIANO'S *face raptly)* The fighting is over. . . .
She kisses him. EMILIANO'S *arms go around her tightly, and they stand there, locked in embrace. The* MOTHER *opens her mouth to protest, but nothing comes out. She looks at the* AUNT, *who is fanning herself as she watches* EMILIANO *and* JOSEFA.

Medium Shot at Windows

Rejoicing faces of WOMEN, MEN, *and* CHILDREN, *are poked in through the windows,* CHEERING *happily.*

Exterior, the Church

The door opens and out comes SEÑOR ESPEJO, *dressed to the teeth, followed by the* WEDDING PROCESSION. *He has taken it on himself to clear a passage through the* CROWD OF ZAPATISTA FIGHTERS *and* VILLAGE PEOPLE *for the bride and groom,* EMILIANO *and* JOSEFA. *The* PROCESSION *passes through a double line of* GUERRILLA FIGHTERS *in white field clothes who present arms in a highly irregular salute. . . . As the* WEDDING PARTY *passes, the* MEN *behind break ranks and follow. . . .*

Dissolve to:
Interior, Room—Large Brass Bed

All alone lies JOSEFA *in her nightgown.* RIFLE FIRE OUTSIDE. JOSEFA *awakes. She is alone in bed.* AN-OTHER COUPLE OF SHOTS. *She looks around . . . hears* EMILIANO'S LAUGHTER.

JOSEFA: Emiliano . . . ?

EMILIANO *at the window is* LAUGHING, *looking out.*

EMILIANO: It's almost morning. They never get tired. . . .

JOSEFA *gets out of bed and goes over to the window . . . and looks down.*

Exterior, Courtyard from Their Angle—Night

The ruins of the feast tables, wine, spilled food all over everything and a gallant little band of DRUNKS, *among them* EUFEMIO, FERNANDO, PABLO, *still holding forth.*

Emiliano and Josefa at the Window

JOSEFA: Come back to bed, Emiliano. . . .

Group at Table in Courtyard

In the midst of throwing his head back to SING LOUDER, EUFEMIO *sees them in the window. He stops in his song.*

EUFEMIO: Emiliano, my brother. Josefa, my sister!

Full of love for everybody he turns to an old and ugly battle-scarred VETERAN, *sitting next to him.*

EUFEMIO: My darling friend. *(weeps)* We're getting old. *(a closer look)* We're getting *very* old.

> The OLD WARRIOR *bends over on the table and he too cries.* EUFEMIO *looks for new fields to love. Next to him, cold sober, is* FERNANDO.

EUFEMIO: I know what's the matter with you. You are unhappy because the fighting is over.

FERNANDO *(*MUTTERING *to himself)*: Half victories! All this celebrating and nothing really won!

EUFEMIO *(embracing him)*: I love you—but I don't like you. I've never liked you.

FERNANDO *(still going on)*: There will have to be a lot more blood shed.

EUFEMIO *(losing patience with him)*: All right! There *will* be! But not tonight! *(gives him bottle)* Here—enjoy yourself! Be human!

Interior, Bedroom

> JOSEFA *goes back to bed. She* CALLS SOFTLY.

JOSEFA: Emiliano!

> *He goes to the bed and sits on the edge.*

JOSEFA: You're restless. *(no answer)* Are you unhappy?

EMILIANO: No! Go to sleep.

JOSEFA: Can't you sleep?

EMILIANO: Pretty soon.

JOSEFA: What are you thinking?

EMILIANO: I'm not thinking anything.

JOSEFA: You are too. I know all about it. I've been married to hundreds of generals. Emiliano!

> *Suddenly she throws a pillow at him. This brings him around.*

EMILIANO: Yes.

JOSEFA: What are you worried about? We'll find a good piece of land somewhere and we'll settle down. You'll raise horses and you'll raise melons, and you'll raise me.

EMILIANO: And I will buy you two new dresses—both beautiful. *(he kisses her)* Go to sleep now.

JOSEFA: I don't want to sleep! *(suddenly, serious)* Emiliano, the fighting *is* over?

EMILIANO: Yes. Madero is in the Capitol. Tomorrow, I'll go see him. It's over.

JOSEFA: Can I go with you?

EMILIANO: No.

JOSEFA *(quickly, without transition)*: Do you think we'll have children?

EMILIANO *(just as quickly)*: Of course.

JOSEFA: We'll name them all Francisco after Madero because he brought peace.

EMILIANO *is pacing the floor like a polar bear in a cage.*

JOSEFA: Emiliano? *(no answer)* Is it something about me?

EMILIANO *goes over to her tenderly.*

EMILIANO: No, no Josefa . . . don't think that.

JOSEFA *(no longer playing)*: Then I want you to tell me. . . .

EMILIANO: I'll see Madero and the men around him. . . .

JOSEFA: You're not telling me.

EMILIANO *(continuing)*: Men from the schools, lawyers, strangers . . . Educated men . . .

JOSEFA: Emiliano you're not telling me.

EMILIANO: A horse and a rifle won't help me there!

Suddenly he looks keenly at her. He goes closer to her, whispers in her ear, as if ashamed of himself.

EMILIANO *(WHISPERING)*: I can't read.

She looks at him with understanding and love.

EMILIANO *(continuing)*: Teach me.

JOSEFA: Of course. . . .

EMILIANO *(with growing excitement)*: Teach me now. Get a book. . . . Now!

Noise of a drunken party outside. . . . EMILIANO goes to the window and leans out.

EMILIANO: Go away! Get out! Can't you let a man sleep on his wedding night?

He turns back to the bed. JOSEFA has a large open

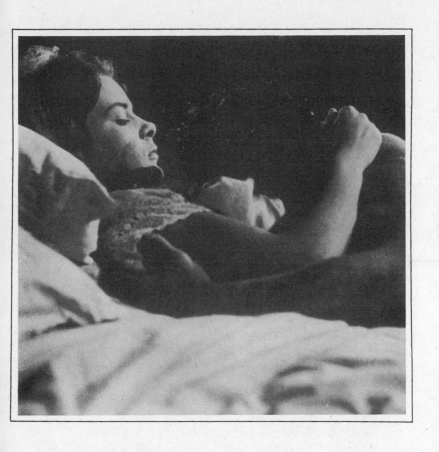

book in front of her. EMILIANO *sits down beside her. They look like two children.* . . .

EMILIANO: Begin!!

Dissolve to:
Full Shot—Interior, a Government Office in Mexico City

It is in a state of confusion. MEN *are moving filing cabinets. There is the characteristic constant repair that is invariable in Mexico; this always involves* HAMMERING. *On one side a* WORKMAN *is measuring a pane for replacement, and we see that there is a bullet hole in the glass. We discover* FRANCISCO MADERO *pointing to a large map on the floor, around which stand* EMILIANO *and* FERNANDO.

MADERO: Díaz was rottener than we knew. When Huerta pushed from the north, with Pancho Villa's help . . . and you, General, from the south, why Díaz crumbled.

EMILIANO *(very humbly)*: If you will forgive me, sir, when will the village lands be given back? The country people are asking.

MADERO: Now we must build—slowly and carefully!

EMILIANO: Thank you. . . . But the country people want to know—

MADERO: They will get their land, but under the law. This is a delicate matter. It must be studied.

EMILIANO: What is there to study?

MADERO: The lands must be given back under the law so that there will be no injustice. And speaking of lands, let me show you this. *(he turns to his desk, riffles through a number of maps, pulls out one and lays it on top)* You see here, where these two streams meet? The land is very rich here, rich and level and well watered . . . and I'm told it has a good house on it. . . . Do you know what this is, General?

EMILIANO: No, sir. . . .

MADERO: This is your ranch and no one deserves it more than you.

70

EMILIANO: *My* ranch?

MADERO: Yes. It is a fine old custom to reward victorious generals . . .

> *Suddenly with a tremendous violence* EMILIANO BANGS *his gun on the floor.* . . .

EMILIANO: I did not fight for a ranch!

MADERO *(quickly)*: I don't think you know what I meant.

EMILIANO *(topping him)* I know what you meant. . . .

> *Now he tries hard to get control of himself. Then he* SPEAKS . . . *with difficulty.*

EMILIANO: Pardon me, sir. . . . But the land I fought for was not for myself!

MADERO: But General—

EMILIANO: What are you going to do about the land I did fight for?

MADERO: General . . . General . . . that will be taken care of, believe me, in good time.

EMILIANO: *Now* is a good time!

MADERO: General Zapata, sit down.

EMILIANO: I'm not tired.

MADERO: This is a constitutional government, there is only one way to do these—*(there is a tremendous* HAMMERING*)* I can't think! I can't think here! This confusion! Get out . . . get out!

> *He goes to the* MAN *fixing a window and drags him to the door, herds the* OTHERS *out . . . stops a* MAN *with a paper.* . . .

MADERO: Give me these. I'll sign these now. Don't let anybody else in. . . .

Another Part of the Room—Eufemio and Pablo

> EMILIANO, *followed by* FERNANDO, *walks toward them.*

EMILIANO: This mouse in the black suit talks too much like Díaz.

PABLO: No, he's right. This is peace. We must work by law now.

FERNANDO: Law? Laws don't govern. Men do. And the

same men who governed before are here now, in that room. They have his ear—it's obvious. They must be cleaned out. . . .

EMILIANO: First, I want the land given back . . .

FERNANDO: And if Madero doesn't do it—

EMILIANO: Yes?

FERNANDO: Then he is an enemy, too.

PABLO: But you're his emissary, his officer, his friend. . . .

FERNANDO: I'm a friend to no one—and to nothing except logic. . . . This is the time for killing!

EMILIANO: Peace is very difficult.

During the foregoing EUFEMIO *has turned aside, is standing by the map on the desk.* EMILIANO *steps over to him.*

EMILIANO *(to* EUFEMIO*)*: What do you think?

EUFEMIO *(*SOTTO VOCE*)*: That's a nice piece of land he offered you. . . . What's the harm? You've never taken anything. And what have you got? Nothing!

Wider Angle

The room has grown quiet. . . . MADERO *comes toward them.*

MADERO: Now it's quiet. *(sinks wearily in his chair)* General Zapata—do you trust me?

Close Shot—Emiliano, silent.

Fernando and Pablo looking at Emiliano.

Eufemio, staring at his brother.

Group Shot—around Madero

MADERO: You must trust me! I promise you that my first preoccupation is with the land, but in a way that is permanent. But, before we can do anything by law, we must have law. We cannot have an armed and angry nation. . . . It is time, General, to stack our arms . . . in fact,

that is the first step. . . . That is my first request of you.
. . . Stack your arms and disband your army.

EMILIANO: And who'll enforce the laws when we have them?

MADERO: The regular army. The police!

EMILIANO: But they're the ones we just fought and beat!
Now EMILIANO *picks up his rifle, advances slowly toward* MADERO.

EMILIANO: Give me your watch!

MADERO: What?

EMILIANO: Give me your watch.
This is an order. Fiercely given and meant. MADERO *slowly removes his watch from his breast pocket and holds it out.* EMILIANO *takes it, looks at it.*

EMILIANO: It's a beautiful watch . . . expensive. . . . *(now quickly)* Now, take my rifle.
He reverses his gun and offers it. MADERO *does not take it.* ZAPATA *lays the gun on the desk, with the barrel pointing toward his own chest.*

EMILIANO: Now . . . you can take your watch back. . . .
but without that—*(he points to the gun)* Could you?

MADERO *(chuckling)*: You draw a strong moral . . .

EMILIANO: You ask us to disarm . . . are you sure we could get our land back, or keep it, if we disarm?

MADERO: It's not that simple, there's the matter of time.

EMILIANO: Time . . . yes, time . . . time is one thing for a lawmaker, but to a farmer there is a time to plant and a time to harvest. . . . You cannot plant in harvest time.

MADERO: General Zapata, do you trust me?

EMILIANO: Just the way my people trust me. I trust you and they trust me as long as we keep our promises.
(reaches for his gun) Not a moment longer.
He thinks a moment, turns, and starts toward the door. FERNANDO, PABLO, *and* EUFEMIO *follow.*

MADERO: Where are you going?

EMILIANO: I'm going home.

MADERO: What will you do there?

EMILIANO: I'll wait. But not for long!
The door closes on THE FOUR.

Another Door to the Room

It opens and there enters a MAN *we have not seen before. He is* VICTORIANO HUERTA, *one of* MADERO's *generals from the north. A hard, cruel, ambitious man. An aide now steps in behind him.* HUERTA *starts forward.*

Angle at Madero's Desk, *as Huerta enters, followed by several tough, hardened Generals. As the scene progresses, they gradually step in near to Madero, so that they seem to be surrounding him.*

HUERTA: Kill that Zapata now. Save time, lives, perhaps your own.

MADERO: Were you listening, General Huerta?

HUERTA: I advise you to shoot Zapata now.

MADERO: I don't shoot my own people.

HUERTA: You'll learn ... or you won't learn. ...

MADERO: He's a fine man.

HUERTA: What does that mean?

MADERO: I mean he's an honest man.

HUERTA: What has that got to do with it??!! A man can be honest and completely wrong!

MADERO: I trust him.

HUERTA: To do what? I feel it is essential that I take my troops down to Morelos and help him decide to disarm.
There is a KNOCK *on the door, then the door opens. It is* PABLO. *He sees who's there.*

PABLO: Oh. ...

MADERO: Come in. ...

Angle at Door

PABLO *looks at* HUERTA *uncertainly.* . . . *He hesitates, still by the door.* MADERO *crosses over to him warmly.* . . .

PABLO *(to* MADERO*)*: I thought—

74

HUERTA: You can speak freely.

MADERO: I want to speak to General Zapata again. . . . Ask him to come back, will you?

PABLO: He won't come back. He's stubborn, you know . . . but if you could come down to Morelos, he's different there. You know, his whole life has been fighting. *(SOTTO VOCE)* He can hardly read. *(urgently)* He needs you. He may not know it yet, but he needs you to help him. And he can learn . . . he wants to . . . and, if you'll excuse me, you need him too.

MADERO *thinks for a moment; then looks at* PABLO.

MADERO: I will come. . . .

PABLO: Thank you. *(bows, then formally)* With your permission, sir. . . . *(to* HUERTA*)* Excuse the interruption, please.

This means: "May I leave now?" MADERO *answers by stepping over to* PABLO *and embracing him.*

MADERO: Tell him I will come. . . .

PABLO *exits.* . . . MADERO *turns back to* HUERTA.

MADERO *(to* HUERTA*)*: I will do it *without* troops. . . . Troops are not necessary . . . these are fine men. . . .

MADERO *turns to exit, pauses.*

MADERO: You know General Huerta, there *is* such a thing as an honest man. . . .

MADERO *smiles and exits.*

Close Shot—Huerta and Aide

HUERTA WHOOPS.

HUERTA: What a fool! Oh, the odor of goodness! Give me a drink. . . .

The AIDE *gets out a bottle.* . . .

HUERTA: We'll never get any place as long as Zapata is alive. He *believes* in what he's fighting for. . . .

AIDE: So does Madero, General. . . .

HUERTA: Oh, I know, but he's a mouse . . . he can be handled. . . . Zapata's a tiger . . . you have to kill a tiger!

CAMERA MOVES DOWNWARD, *and we see that* HUERTA

*is standing on the map, his feet firmly planted on the
State of Morelos.*

Dissolve to:
Exterior, the Plaza of a Town

In front of a table where there are CLERKS, *slowly
passes a line of* ZAPATISTA FIGHTERS *surrendering their
guns. As the weapons are surrendered, the name of
each owner is written in a book and on a tag tied to the
gun. The line stretches all the way across the plaza.*

Medium Shot—Group at Table

*As each man surrenders his weapon it is thrown into
a farm cart. Behind the table stand* EMILIANO, MADERO,
PABLO, *and* EUFEMIO. *(The* SOLDADERA *is in the background.)*

MADERO: You see, they feel all right about giving up their
arms now that I have explained it to them.

PABLO: He explained it very well, didn't he, Emiliano?

EMILIANO *is silent.* MADERO *watches him.*

MADERO: They've accepted it. Have you?

EMILIANO: I've been fighting so long. I don't understand
peace.

MADERO: Peace is the hard problem. Many men have
been honest in war. . . . I often wonder how a man can
stay honest under the pressure of peace. . . .

A MAN *in the line who is just about to give up his
rifle, holds it up. . . .*

MAN: Let us keep these.

MADERO *(turns)*: What do you mean?

EUFEMIO: He means, so he can shoot you if you turn
crooked!

He suddenly bursts into crude LAUGHTER *and goes off.
The* MAN *hands over his rifle and moves along.* MADERO
looks at EMILIANO *and they* LAUGH, *too. . . .*

EMILIANO *(he points to a grizzled* OLD MAN *who is next*

in line): He doesn't look like much, but he's one of the best fighters we had. Aren't you, Apolonio?

APOLONIO: No.

He gives up his rifle and moves on. They all LAUGH.

EMILIANO *(to* MADERO*)*: Did I tell you about the little boy who got my horse?

MADERO: Yes, you did. Where is he? I'd like to meet him.

EMILIANO *(throwing it away)*: He's dead. *(thinks a second, then:)* We were never able to find the horse.

Another Angle

EMILIANO *indicates a* WOMAN *who is bringing three rifles. Nods at her with his head.*

MADERO: That woman has three rifles!

EMILIANO: Lost a husband and two sons—killed.

The WOMAN *deposits the guns.* MADERO's *eyes fill with tears. He moves toward the* WOMAN, *reaching in his pockets for something to give her. All he can find is his watch. He hands it to her. She puts her hand under her apron.*

MADERO: Take it!

WOMAN: Oh, no, it is too valuable.

MADERO *takes her hand and puts the watch in the palm and closes the fingers over it and* SAYS, HARSHLY:

MADERO: As valuable as your sons?

CAMERA MOVES INTO CLOSE SHOT *of* EMILIANO *and* PABLO. *We see that* EMILIANO *likes and believes in* MADERO. PABLO *sees this and is glad.*

Wider Angle

FERNANDO, *followed by* EUFEMIO, *comes into the scene, and gestures to* EMILIANO.

FERNANDO *(anxiously)*: Emiliano, come here!

EMILIANO: What do you want?

FERNANDO *(changes his mind. Speaks sullenly, gesturing toward* MADERO*)*: Ask *him!*

EMILIANO: Use respect!

77

MADERO *(with a gesture of helplessness)*: What is it . . . ?

EUFEMIO: General Huerta's forces are coming through the pass!

FERNANDO *(to* MADERO*)*: Pretend you don't know it!

MADERO: Oh, no, they're not—no, they can't!

EMILIANO *(to* FERNANDO*)*: How do you know?

FERNANDO *points to three dusty and perspiring* SCOUTS *who are drinking water thirstily.*

EUFEMIO: The Scouts! Three regiments with artillery.

EMILIANO: Who posted Scouts?

FERNANDO: I did.

EMILIANO: You?

FERNANDO *(indicating* MADERO*)*: I don't trust him. And I'm right! Look at him!

MADERO *is bewildered. The* OTHERS *stare at him. A* CITIZEN, *unaware of what is happening, approaches* MADERO.

CITIZEN *(to* MADERO*)*: I want to shake the hand of our Liberator. I can tell my children.

Automatically, MADERO *extends his hand.*

MADERO *(as though to himself)*: Troops are coming, Huerta has disobeyed orders. . . .

CITIZEN: What—what do you say, sir?

MADERO: Thank you very much. *(the* CITIZEN *goes)* I'll have to go and stop them. Huerta wouldn't dare.

He rises, walks away a few steps, hesitates—confused and bewildered.

FERNANDO *(to* EMILIANO*)*: Don't let him get away!

PABLO: You *must* trust Madero, Emiliano! He can bring us peace.

FERNANDO *(interrupting)*: Peace! . . . Three regiments coming down on us! Peace! You ugly little ape, you fool!

PABLO *goes for his knife and for* FERNANDO's *neck. . . . A knife has suddenly appeared in the hands of the* SOLDADERA.

EMILIANO: Pablo! Stop it! Put that knife away! Fernando, send cavalry to engage—see to the outposts. . . .

FERNANDO: Yes, General. . . . *(starts away, stops—to* MADERO*)* Go on back to Mexico City. . . . Huerta is a strong man . . . he'll gobble you up. . . .

EMILIANO *interrupts violently.*

EMILIANO: Fernando!

FERNANDO *exits.* . . .

EMILIANO: Pablo! The snipers. Flank the road. . . .

EUFEMIO *(*SOTTO VOCE, *indicating* MADERO*)*: Might be a good idea to finish him off! What do you say?

Before EMILIANO *can reply,* MADERO *comes back to him.*

MADERO: Emiliano, believe in me! I will stop the troops.

EMILIANO: I hope so. . . . But if you can't, I will! *(to* EUFEMIO*)* Come on.

They exit.

Another Angle

EMILIANO *is issuing orders. The line reverses. Guns are issued. An electric quality comes into the square like a storm breaking.* HORSES *and* RIDERS *move about with great speed.*

Medium Shot—Madero and Pablo (the Soldadera in the background).

MADERO *nervously wipes his forehead.* PABLO *looks at him sympathetically.*

MADERO: General Huerta must have misunderstood.

PABLO: I'll talk to Emiliano. I'll bring you two together again. . . .

He hurries off, followed by the SOLDADERA. MADERO *still stands there, confused and bewildered.*

Dissolve to:

Long Shot—Mounted Federal Scout, *coming down a road which leads to a river.*

Medium Shot—*the Scout as he stops at the edge of the river, looks carefully in all directions; then he turns in his saddle, signals in the direction of a heavily wooded area.*

Long Shot—Shooting toward the Wooded Area

A mounted FEDERAL COLUMN *emerges from the woods, comes toward the river.*

Full Shot of the Column Crossing the River.

As they are in the middle of the stream, suddenly they are FIRED UPON. *There is a wild thrashing about of the frightened* HORSES. *The* FEDERALES *look around, trying to find out where the firing is coming from.*

Another Angle around the River.

From the tall grass the figures of the ZAPATISTAS *rise, continue* FIRING. *At the height of this battle, we* CUT TO:

Close Shot—Emiliano

on horseback, his field glasses held to his eyes, watching the battle. He lowers the glasses, and a look of satisfaction comes over his face. The way he planned it, that way it worked!

Dissolve to:
A Small Room in the National Palace—Mexico City

It is sparsely but adequately furnished. TWO SOLDIERS *stand at the door guarding it. At a bare table sits* MADERO, *staring straight ahead. He's in a highly nervous state . . . almost hysteria.*

There's a KNOCK *at the door. The* TWO SOLDIERS *open it a slit, and then, seeing who it is, open it wide. An immaculately dressed* SENIOR OFFICER *enters.* MADERO *almost runs to him.*

MADERO: Did you see him? Did you see Huerta?

OFFICER: Yes, my President. . . .

MADERO: How does he explain this? Why am I a prisoner here?

OFFICER *(sauvely)*: You're no longer a prisoner, my President.

80

MADERO: But they won't let me leave! I've been in this room for days!

OFFICER: Of course. He's guarding you for your safety. You have enemies outside.

MADERO: What enemies?

OFFICER: Zapata, Pancho Villa, they've all turned against you. But don't worry. General Huerta loves you. He will protect you. You must agree—here you have been safe.

MADERO: Why doesn't he give me safe conduct to the Port? When is he going to let me see him?

OFFICER: Tonight. He asked me to take you to him.

Frantically MADERO *runs to a mirror. We watch him* CLOSE UP *as he ties his cravat, straightens his worn hair. . . .*

Dissolve to:
A Military Car with a Driver

In the back seat, HUERTA *and an* AIDE, *smoking cigars.* HUERTA *looks at a watch.*

HUERTA: They are late.

A SOLDIER *runs up to the car.*

SOLDIER: They're coming. . . .

HUERTA *throws away his cigar. Looks out the window of the car.*

An Open Car Drives into View, Its Lights Dimmed

In the back seat between TWO OFFICERS *sits* MADERO. *His face is full of anticipation. The car stops;* MADERO *looks around questioningly at an* OFFICER.

OFFICER: Get out.

MADERO: Is he here?

OFFICER: Get out.

MADERO *raises his head and sees the wall of the penitentiary, before which the scene is being played.*

Suddenly the whole plot and all knowledge of it, crashes in on his mind.

81

Close-up—Madero.

He knows he's doomed.

Wider Angle

Suddenly the TWO OFFICERS *give him a boost.* MADERO *seems to accept his fate. Almost aloofly he steps from the car.* TWO SOLDIERS *appear from the darkness, take him by the arms and conduct him almost gently in front of the car. They leave him. Suddenly the full headlights turn on him. They blind him. He looks around, for where to go. . . . Takes a few tentative steps . . . turns back toward the car and starts to* SPEAK. . . .

MADERO: My friend, what—

The EXTRA LOUD HORN *of the car* SOUNDS, *drowning out his* VOICE. MADERO *turns away hopelessly, his body waits for the bullets he knows are coming.*

Huerta's Car

HUERTA *is listening tensely. . . . There is a* VOLLEY OF SHOTS *offscreen. The* SOUND *of the automobile* HORN DIES OUT. *The open car, in which* MADERO *came, crosses behind.*

HUERTA *(to his* AIDE*)*: So much for the mouse. Now we'll go for the TIGER.

He takes a fresh cigar, bites off the end of it.

Dissolve to:
Zapata's Headquarters—the Courtyard of a Ruined Hacienda

A court-martial is taking place. ZAPATA, *looking much older and much more worn, is sitting at a table. Behind him stands* FERNANDO, *who looks fiercer and meaner. All around in a great circle stand the* MEN *of his army listening. They are really battle-worn. A high wind is blowing.* EUFEMIO *is conducting the court-martial.*

Medium Shot—at Table

ZAPATA *looks at a* GUARDED MAN, *who stands in front of the table.*

CLERK OF THE COURT: Consorting with the enemy. He was seen talking to an officer of Huerta's army.

EUFEMIO *(leaning toward* PRISONER*)*: We were ambushed. We *know* that now! What have you got to say for yourself?

PRISONER *(with a certain amount of arrogance)*: Why shouldn't I talk to him? He was my brother-in-law. He brought me a message from my wife.

EUFEMIO: How did he know where to find you?

PRISONER *(pause—he is trapped)*: I sent word.

EUFEMIO *(rising)*: You sent word and we were ambushed!

PRISONER *(again defensive)*: I haven't seen my wife in two years!

EUFEMIO *(to* GUARDS*)*: Shoot him!

EMILIANO: Wait a minute.

An electric pause, as they all look toward him. The PRISONER'*s face lights up with hope.*

EMILIANO *(to* PRISONER*)*: Look behind you.

Long Shot

What he sees: A LONG LINE *of white-clad* ZAPATISTAS, *each carrying the body of a* DEAD ZAPATISTA *up a hill (moving away from the* CAMERA*) and disappearing over the brow of the hill.* ANOTHER LINE *comes back, moving toward us.*

Back to Scene

ZAPATA: Two hundred and forty-four fighting men. We planned a surprise. Huerta was ready for us. *(he* SPEAKS *to* ALL THE MEN*)* When they killed Madero, we had to start all over again. We lost many men. It was necessary. But *this* was useless. Two hundred and forty-four good farmers, your relatives, with victory in their mouths, will never chew it. *(to the* PRISONER, *with sudden violence)* Now do you see why we have *hard* discipline? You told your wife where we would be—and—*(he turns to* EUFEMIO*)* Shoot him.

The PRISONER *is led away.* EMILIANO *looks up and sees a group of* FEDERAL SOLDIERS *under guard.*

CAPTAIN OF THE GUARD: Thirty-two deserters, my General. They want to come over to us. . . .

EMILIANO *(he has said this many times recently, there have been many* DESERTERS *to him)*: If you want to fight for your land and your liberty, you're welcome. You'll be watched. There's no mercy for traitors. None! It's easier to come over to us now that we are winning, isn't it? *(to* FERNANDO*)* Take care of them.

FERNANDO *gestures to another* MAN, *who comes forward and escorts the* DESERTERS *away.*

EMILIANO *(to* EUFEMIO*)*: Go on.

EUFEMIO *(to* CLERK*)*: Next!

A PRISONER *is brought forward.*

CLERK: This one broke our law against looting.

EMILIANO *(rising, to* EUFEMIO*)*: I'll sleep a little.

He takes from EUFEMIO *a bottle of strong liquor (which* EUFEMIO *has been liberally using). He goes off,* FERNANDO *follows him.*

Moving Shot—Emiliano and Fernando

FERNANDO *watches him.*

FERNANDO: Putting it off?

They go up to a door opening in the thick wall and enter. CAMERA STOPS *on the* SOLDADERA, *who is squatting against the wall on the side of the door. Her face, as ever, is expressionless. By now she is really worn. Much time and misery have passed. In her* rebozo, *slung over one shoulder, lies an* INFANT. *She pays no attention to it. . . . She is making tortillas. She doesn't look up as the* MEN *go by.*

85

PABLO *is sitting on a bench with a* GUARD *on either side of him. He looks up as* EMILIANO *and* FERNANDO *enter.* EMILIANO *takes a seat, avoids* PABLO'S *glance.*

PABLO: You look tired, Emiliano.

EMILIANO *doesn't answer.* FERNANDO *takes charge.*

FERNANDO: He met with the enemy: I have witnesses!

In the scene that follows, FERNANDO ADDRESSES PABLO, *but* PABLO *never talks to* FERNANDO *nor looks at him. He* SPEAKS *to* EMILIANO.

PABLO: You don't need witnesses, Emiliano. Just ask me. It's true I met Madero before he was killed.

FERNANDO: You met him many times!

PABLO: Many times, Emiliano.

FERNANDO: Even after Madero had signed orders to destroy us!

PABLO: That was at the end, Emiliano. Madero wasn't himself. He was trying to hold Huerta in check. Then Huerta killed him. He was a good man, Emiliano. He wanted to build houses and plant fields. And he was right. If we could begin to build—even while the burning goes on. If we could plant while we destroy . . .

FERNANDO: This is your defense?

SOUND *of execution offstage.*

PABLO: You and Villa will beat Huerta, soon! But then, there will be other Huertas, always other Huertas! Killing only makes new enemies, Emiliano. . . .

FERNANDO: You deserted our cause!

PABLO: Our cause was land—not a thought, but corn-planted earth to feed the families. And Liberty—not a word, but man sitting safely in front of his house in the evening. And Peace—not a dream, but a time of rest and kindness. The question beats in my head, Emiliano. Can a good thing come from a bad act? Can peace come from so much killing? Can kindness finally come from so much violence? *(he looks now directly into* EMILIANO'S *immobile eyes)* And can a man whose thoughts are born in anger and hatred, can such a man lead to peace? And govern in peace? I don't know, Emiliano. You must have thought of it. Do you know? Do you know?

Silence. EMILIANO *does not answer. A pause . . . off-screen—a* FUSILLADE *is* HEARD. *The* EXECUTION SQUAD. FERNANDO *looks at* EMILIANO.

FERNANDO *(slowly):* Two hundred and forty-four of our fighting men were killed this morning. We planned to surprise the enemy. They surprised us!

Pause.

Close Shot—Emiliano and Pablo

PABLO *(sensing what is happening behind* EMILIANO'S *mask):* Emiliano, we've been friends since we guarded the corn against the blackbirds.

EMILIANO *(slowly):* You knew our rule against consorting with the enemy?

PABLO: Yes, my General.

EMILIANO: And yet you ignored it?

PABLO: Yes, my General.

FERNANDO'S VOICE: Shall I call the squad?

PABLO *(with pleading in his eyes):* Emiliano, not strangers. Do it yourself. Do it yourself!

FERNANDO *gets up, silently, and goes outside.*

Full Shot—Room

FERNANDO *gestures to the* TWO GUARDS, *who leave.* FERNANDO *follows.* EMILIANO *and* PABLO *are alone.*

Exterior, Small Dark Room

FERNANDO *comes out, closes the door.*

Closeup—Soldadera

She looks up at him for a moment.

Back to Scene

FERNANDO *stands just outside the door to the small dark room. A* COURIER, *guarded, comes up.*

COURIER (*to* FERNANDO): Where's General Zapata? I have a message of great importance from General Villa.
FERNANDO: General Zapata is busy.

From inside comes the SOUND *of* A SHOT. *The* SOLDADERA *dumps the charcoal from her brazier; she stands up and, gathering her food, walks away.*

FERNANDO (*to* COURIER): General Zapata will see you now.

Fade out

Fade in:
Emiliano's and Josefa's Home—Night—Josefa and Señor Espejo

It is poor. Against one wall is the brass marriage bed. A small altar is against another wall. In the center of the room is a table and two primitive chairs. A candle burns on the table. On one side of the table JOSEFA *is working . . . on the other the* FATHER *gulps beans and lectures her, gesturing with his spoon for emphasis. At the same time he is reading a newspaper.*

SEÑOR ESPEJO: Tell me: Why is he a general at all? What has he got from it? Look at you. Look at that dress! Is this a general's house? Pancho Villa knows what to do with his opportunities. Look how *he* dresses!

Insert—the Newspaper

A picture of PANCHO VILLA *in full-dress uniform in shiny boots.*

Back to Scene

SEÑOR ESPEJO (*mouth full of beans, to* JOSEFA, *who has looked over at him*): Don't argue with me! I know. Being a general is a business opportunity, and he's not taking advantage of it. He could take half the state and everyone would respect him for it, and he won't touch it. . . . (*with sudden violence*) I give up on him! Never had any faith in him. . . . *(suddenly)* What's that? Do you hear horses . . . ?

> *The door opens and* EMILIANO *walks right in. . . . Outside, his* ESCORT *can be* HEARD *dismounting, tying* HORSES, *etc.* JOSEFA *gets up and goes to him. He strokes her hair . . . her cheeks. She sees something desperate in his face.*

JOSEFA: Are you hurt?

EMILIANO: No.

JOSEFA: How did you get through the lines?

EMILIANO: There are no lines. Huerta's army is beaten. Villa has entered Mexico City. . . . I'll meet him there.

> JOSEFA *is helping him take off his equipment. . . .*

SEÑOR ESPEJO: Congratulation, my General!!

> ZAPATA *just looks at him. He seems deeply bitter.* JOSEFA *sees this. . . .*

JOSEFA: Are you sick?

EMILIANO: No . . . tired. . . . Tired. . . .

JOSEFA: But something's wrong . . . ?

EMILIANO: No. We've won. Nothing's wrong. I need sleep. . . . Let me sleep. . . .

[SEÑOR ESPEJO: Before you go to Mexico City—my son —I'd like to have a talk with you. . . .

JOSEFA: Father . . . !

SEÑOR ESPEJO: About business conditions.

> JOSEFA *takes her* FATHER *by the elbow and leads him toward the door. . . .*

JOSEFA: Father. . . .

Close Shot—at Door

SEÑOR ESPEJO *(*WHISPERING *in the doorway)*: Don't let him miss this chance. He can be President. Villa's not so smart. . . . When he gets rested I want to have a practical talk with him.

> *She puts him out the door. Just as she's closing it:*

SEÑOR ESPEJO: He needs some practical advice.

Interior, Room

> *She crosses over to* EMILIANO, *who is lying down on the bed in exhaustion. . . . He smiles at her.*

EMILIANO: Why is it that since your father has come to adore me I can't stand him? When he had no use for me I rather respected him.

JOSEFA: You can *still* respect him.

> *She kisses him.*

Dissolve to:

Exterior, Their House—Night—Late

> The GUARDS' *campfire. . . . They are asleep.* SOUND *of* DOGS BARKING. ONE *of the* GUARDS *lifts up out of his sleep, looks around, sees and senses nothing, then drops down into sleep again. The silhouetted figure of a* WOMAN *is seen crossing towards the hut of the* ZA-PATAS.

Interior, Hut, lit only by a votive candle.

> *The door to the outside is stealthily opened and the figure of a* WOMAN *steals in, closing the door. We can not see her for a moment, then suddenly she is very close to us. We see who it is:* PABLO's SOLDADERA. *We* PAN *her over to where* ZAPATA *is sleeping.* JOSEFA *awakens, sees the* CREEPING FIGURE. *She leaps toward her. The* SOLDADERA *lunges, her knife striking* JOSEFA's *hand.*

Wider Angle

> JOSEFA *is upon her.* EMILIANO *has just rolled over to avoid her blade. The* GUARDS *rush in and hold her. Lights are lit.* EMILIANO *sees who it is. He stares at her. She at him.*

EMILIANO: You! What is this?

SOLDADERA: Go ahead and shoot me!

EMILIANO *(to* GUARDS*)*: Take her out. . . .

> *The* GUARDS *take her out. She does not struggle.*

90

Medium Shot—Emiliano and Josefa

EMILIANO *stands dazed.* JOSEFA *looks at a cut on her hand.* EMILIANO *notices.*

EMILIANO: She cut you. Let me see.

JOSEFA: It isn't deep.

EMILIANO *pulls his neck scarf off, wraps her hand. Suddenly something seems to quit in him. He collapses in complete despair.*

JOSEFA: Emiliano. . . .

She takes his head in her hands. He is crying from exhaustion and bewilderment and pain.

EMILIANO: My own people. She's from my village.

JOSEFA: She tried to kill you.

EMILIANO: Pablo—Pablo— I've known her since—before Pablo. . . .

JOSEFA: Lie down and sleep. . . .

He pulls himself away from her and walks towards the door as if listening for a shot. Then walks back toward JOSEFA. . . .

JOSEFA: Lie down, you must sleep.

EMILIANO *(SHOUTS)*: It must stop! The killing must stop! Pablo said it. That's all I know how to do!

Exterior, Hut

The campfire has been built up. A GUARD *is taking out his pistol to shoot the* SOLDADERA, *who is on her knees. Many half-dressed* ZAPATISTAS *have come out of the barracks nearby and watch.*

EMILIANO'S VOICE: Get away from her.

She stays on her knees as EMILIANO *enters. He crouches beside her and puts his arm around her.*

Close Shot—Emiliano and the Soldadera

EMILIANO: Look at me!

He turns her around and forces her to look at him.

SOLDADERA *(expressionless)*: He was your friend.

EMILIANO *(a* VIOLENT CRY *of pain)*: I *had* to kill him!

The SOLDADERA *snarls like a cat.*

EMILIANO: He was a traitor.

SOLDADERA: He was your friend.

EMILIANO: There were reasons.

SOLDADERA: No reason!

She spits in his face. He doesn't move.

Wider Angle

EMILIANO *walks away from her. He is close to* ONE OF THE GUARDS, *the one who holds the pistol.*

GUARD: My General. She's crazy. Dangerous and crazy. I will shoot her.

EMILIANO: Let her go.

GUARD: Think, my General, she's dangerous!

EMILIANO: Let her go.

GUARD *(walks up to the* SOLDADERA*)*: Go on. . . . *(she looks at him)* Go on!

She gets up, looks in EMILIANO's *face and walks off . . . no expression on her face. A* GUARD *picks up the* SOLDADERA's *knife, which has been lying on the ground. He holds it out to* EMILIANO, SAYING, *"Here's her knife. . . ."*

Close-up—Emiliano, holding the knife.

We see that it is the little knife which belonged to PABLO. *There are tears in his eyes as he looks at the knife which belonged to his friend.*]

Dissolve to:

Full Shot—Interior, Throne Room at Chapultepec

A large gathering of ROUGH FIGHTING MEN *from* VILLA's *army and* ZAPATA's.

Close Shot—Photographer

He has his camera ready and is waiting for them to get set, so he can take a picture.

Villa and Emiliano

EMILIANO *and* VILLA *embrace each other formally.* VILLA *invites* EMILIANO *to sit in the presidential seat.* EMILIANO *refuses, and invites* VILLA *to sit there. There is a slight argument.* VILLA *shrugs, sits in the presidential throne.* ZAPATA *sits beside him. The* OTHERS *range themselves about.* VILLA *pushes* ZAPATA *a little aside because his hat is obscuring* VILLA's *face.* ZAPATA *takes his hat off. They all* LAUGH. *There is a flash of powder. . . . A* CHEER! *Then* PANDEMONIUM. . . .

Close Shot—Villa and Emiliano

VILLA *leans toward* EMILIANO *and says in a* HOARSE WHISPER:
VILLA: Let's get out of here!
They get up together and start to sneak out. Throughout this scene an ARMY BAND PLAYS *a wild victory march.*

Dissolve to:
Long Shot—a Wooded Area Surrounding a Lake

In the foreground are TWO GUARDS; *one is replacing another. Behind them we see a small lake with beautiful overgrowing trees. In the middle of the lake is a small island . . . and in the clearing on the island are* TWO FIGURES. VILLA *sits on the ground, leaning against a tree.* ZAPATA *is standing, leaning, practically lying against an upright tree. He is very relaxed. At various points around the pond are other* SENTINELS, *like those in the foreground of our scene. Behind them are a circle of* PEOPLE *in white, drawn there out of curiosity or anxiety and concern.*
FIRST GUARD *(who is replacing the* SECOND GUARD*)*: All right, I'll stand now. *(confidentially)* What are they doing?

SECOND GUARD: Still talking. Deciding the fate of Mexico. Let them take their time. It's important!

[*Medium Shot—Villa and Zapata*

We see also another FIGURE *close by—a* LITTLE UR-CHIN GIRL *with her little charcoal brazier. She is silent in the background. She is making tortillas. (*FER-NANDO *is there, too, but not immediately seen.)*

VILLA: Why don't you come up to my country for a visit? It's not as green as yours but it is interesting. You'd like it.

EMILIANO: What do you do there?

VILLA: Hunting and women.

EMILIANO: What is there to hunt?

VILLA: Women.

EMILIANO LAUGHS. *He has "bought"* VILLA. . . . VILLA *eats what the* LITTLE GIRL *has offered him. He doesn't laugh. He means it.*

VILLA (*to the* LITTLE GIRL): These are good. (*to* EMILI-ANO) We have some wild pigs up there, not big, but they're tough. Run in packs. Eat a man right off a horse. The women are little pigs, too. Not so pretty, but they're nice. (*He eats*) They make them better in the north. I mean these—(*he holds up a tamale*) Pretty good. . . .

Overcome with good feeling he reaches into his pocket and pulls out a medal, with ribbon, holds it up to the LITTLE GIRL, *admires it with her, and then hands it to her.*

VILLA: Here. Wear it with pride. It once hung on the chest of a former President of Mexico.

EMILIANO LAUGHS *again. This time* VILLA *joins him.*

Close Shot—Little Girl

as she gravely pins the medal to her chest.

Group Shot

EMILIANO *and* VILLA LAUGH TOGETHER *as they watch the* LITTLE GIRL. *They like each other.*]

94

Wider Angle as Fernando steps forward to the Group.

FERNANDO: Gentlemen, it's past three.

VILLA: You're right, we should be asleep!

FERNANDO: We have a great deal to discuss.

VILLA: What do you think we're doing?

FERNANDO: Political matters.

VILLA *(looks at* FERNANDO *and* BELCHES*)*: I eat too much. . . . I don't have anything to discuss. I've made up my mind. I'm going home. I have a nice ranch up there now. I got something out of the fighting. I'm going to be president of that ranch. In the morning I'll hear roosters instead of bugles. . . . You know somebody took a shot at me this morning . . . somebody I didn't even know.

FERNANDO: What do you propose?

VILLA *(to* EMILIANO, *ignoring* FERNANDO*)*: I've been fighting too long. Lost my appetite for it.

EMILIANO: You mean—you're going home?

VILLA: I'm sick of it. We beat one of them and two more jump up. I used to think it would work.

FERNANDO: What about Mexico?

VILLA: I figured it out. Only one man I trust. *(to* EMILI-ANO*)* Can you read?

EMILIANO *(with a look of pride)*: Yes.

VILLA: You're the President.

EMILIANO *(Violently)*: No!

VILLA *(sleepily)*: Yes, you are. I just appointed you. Sleep on it. You'll see I'm right. *(covers his head and sleeps.* FERNANDO *and* EMILIANO *look at each other.* VILLA *uncovers his head)* There's no one else. Do I look like a president? *(covers his head)*

FERNANDO *(to* EMILIANO*)*: He's right. About himself and about you. There *is* no one else!

Close Shot—Emiliano

An absolutely Indian look. . . .

Dissolve to:
Interior, Government office

EMILIANO ZAPATA *is holding audience.* FERNANDO *stands slightly behind him, his hands full of papers. A* SECRETARY *is in front of the desk. Along the side of the wall sit various* MEN *of different classes: an* OLD GENERAL, *a* FOREIGN DIPLOMAT, *a* CHARRO, *a* DELEGATION *of country people. They are all waiting for an audience with* EMILIANO ZAPATA.

Medium Shot—Emiliano and Staff

The SECRETARY *is* READING.

SECRETARY: Acting on the report that there have been gatherings of disgruntled officers in Sautillo, Colonel Chávez, on your orders, my President, moved in with a troop of cavalry after nightfall. The names of the deceased officers are appended, my President.

EMILIANO: General. I am not President.

FERNANDO: All killed?

SECRETARY: All.

FERNANDO: Telegraph congratulations to Colonel Chávez. [*(turns to the* OLD GENERAL, *and beckons him)* Can we have your report on the enemy?

The OLD GENERAL *comes forward....*

OLD GENERAL: General Carranza is still at Vera Cruz. His forces are intact.

FERNANDO: And General Obregón?

OLD GENERAL: Obregón is dug in at Puebla. He would be hard to dislodge. He's a fine officer. *(he turns to* EMILIANO*)* May I speak, my General?

FERNANDO: Your report is finished.

ZAPATA: Speak.

OLD GENERAL: I don't want to support men who have been against you. But Carranza and Obregón are strong, clever, resourceful, and really *quite honest.* Good officers, as you know. Would it seem presumptuous, my

General, to suggest that you consider an alliance with them, for the good of Mexico?

FERNANDO *(violently)*: For the good of Mexico! Madero made an alliance with Huerta for the good of Mexico and Huerta killed him! There are no good alliances! We hunt them down and kill them or they hunt us down and kill us. Díaz did not make alliances and he ruled for thirty-five years.

OLD GENERAL: But Díaz was a dictator.

FERNANDO: The principle of successful rule is always the same. There can be no opposition. Of course, our ends are different.

The OLD GENERAL *hesitates. He knows he is taking his life in his hands. . . . Then he* SPEAKS *to* ZAPATA.

OLD GENERAL: I don't believe that. . . . Do you, my General?

ZAPATA *does not answer him. He is looking straight ahead.*

Close Shot—Old General

OLD GENERAL: I am old and I may be foolish. I have killed so many men who differed with me. I've forgotten why, except that they opposed. And I've forgotten why that, too. You know how time goes . . . and always there were just as many left who opposed. My friends, some-where, sometime, we must start building for peace. As an old soldier I have learned that there are times when you *must* fight. But unless the purpose is peace, the road is endless, the journey empty.

Close-up—Fernando

His eyes are blazing with hostility.

Close Shot—Emiliano's Staff

They drop their eyes before the OLD GENERAL's *stare.*

Close-up—Emiliano

He is looking straight ahead as if he didn't see the OLD GENERAL.

Group Shot

OLD GENERAL *(to* EMILIANO*)*: With your permission, my General. . . .

EMILIANO *has been looking at him sharply. Now he nods. The* OLD GENERAL *starts out.*

Two Shot—Emiliano and Fernando

FERNANDO *(to* EMILIANO *in a* WHISPER*)*: That man is dangerous!

EMILIANO: General. . . .

Close Shot—Old General—at Door

The OLD GENERAL *stops just at the exit door. . . .*

EMILIANO'S VOICE: Thank you.

The OLD GENERAL *smiles a rather sad smile, bows, and goes out.*]

Group Shot—Around Emiliano

EMILIANO *is affected by the* OLD GENERAL'*s smile.*

FERNANDO *(briskly)*: What next?

SECRETARY: A delegation from Morelos with a petition, my———my General. Here's the list of names. *(hands him list)*

EMILIANO *glances at the names. . . .*

EMILIANO: Why, I know some of these . . .

He looks up. For the first time his eyes light up as the DELEGATION *enters.*

EMILIANO: Carlito—Pepe—and you, Lazaro, what are you doing here? What do you want . . . ? What can I do for you?

Delegation Just Inside Door of Room

A young, dark CHARRO *stands in their midst. He has an insolence about him—just as* EMILIANO *had in the scene with* DÍAZ *at the opening of this screenplay.*

LAZARO (to EMILIANO): We have a complaint against your brother.

Close-up—Emiliano

He freezes; his eyes lower.

Medium Shot—Delegation at Door all trying to voice the complaint.

VOICES: Your brother moved into the hacienda at Ayala. . . . He took the land you just distributed. . . . He's living there. . . . He kicked us out. . . . He killed a man who wouldn't go. . . .

Close Shot—Emiliano, looking off toward the Delegation.

EMILIANO: Is this true?
AN OLD INDIAN'S VOICE: Yes, my General.
EMILIANO (stalling): Well, we'll have to do something about that. We'll need a little time. . . .

Wider Angle

The young CHARRO *comes close to* EMILIANO *and* SPEAKS *for the first time. What follows should be reminiscent of the opening scenes of this screenplay.*

CHARRO: These men haven't *got* time!
EMILIANO: But—
CHARRO (holding up his hand for silence): They plowed the land. And they've got it half sowed.
EMILIANO: Did you have any land there . . . ?
CHARRO (insolently): No.
EMILIANO: Then what are you doing here?
CHARRO: These are my neighbors. I can read and write. I wrote the letter for the appointment.
EMILIANO: Neighbors. . . . My brother is a general. He became a general by fighting for many years and killing many of your enemies. Let's not forget that now. (he turns away from the CHARRO, speaks past him to the DELEGATION) You can trust me. I'm one of you, I was—

CHARRO (*continuing*): Since you are, you ought to know that the land can't wait. The furrows are open. The seeds not planted. Stomachs can't wait either.

EMILIANO (*with sudden anger*): What's your name . . . ?

CHARRO: Hernandez. H-E-R——

EMILIANO: I have it.

Insert—Emiliano's Hand

On the list of names he is slowly circling a name . . . exactly as DÍAZ *did his early in our story.*

Close Shot—Emiliano

Suddenly an electric shock goes through him. He stares at the paper. His hand is still making a little circle above the paper. He holds the pencil up . . . point in the air . . . suddenly his thumb moves in a spasm, and the pencil breaks. He drops the pencil . . . picks up the paper with a gesture of violence and crunches it . . . and drops it on the floor.

[Wider Angle—Taking in Delegation

EMILIANO *is like a man in a trance. Slowly he crosses to the* CHARRO. *The* INDIANS *pull back, but the* CHARRO *stands his ground with a little fear in his eyes. There's a feeling of coming murder in the room. When he gets to the* CHARRO, ZAPATA *raises his hand very slowly, and with tenderness, puts it on the* CHARRO's *shoulder. Then he looks blindly around the room, sees his hat on an ornate hatrack. He goes to it, and puts it on.*]

Two Shot—Emiliano and Fernando

FERNANDO: Where are you going?

EMILIANO: I'm going home. . . . I'm going home. There are some things I forgot.

FERNANDO: So you're throwing it away. Leave tonight and your enemies will be here tomorrow—in this room—at that desk! They won't walk away. They'll hunt you

down . . . and you'll get your rest in the sun with the flies in your face. I promise you you won't live long.

EMILIANO: I won't live long anyway. . . .

FERNANDO: Zapata—in the name of all we fought for, don't leave here!

EMILIANO: In the name of all I fought for, I'm going.

FERNANDO: If you leave now—I won't go with you. . . .

EMILIANO: I don't expect you to. . . .

FERNANDO: Thousands of men have died to give you power and you're throwing it away.

EMILIANO: I'm taking it back where it belongs; to thousands of men.

FERNANDO: I won't go with you.

EMILIANO: I don't want you.

He turns abruptly, stares at FERNANDO.

EMILIANO: Now I know you. No wife, no woman, no home, no field. You do not gamble, drink, no friends, no love. . . . You only destroy. . . . I guess that's your love. . . . And I'll tell you what you will do now! You will go to Obregón or Carranza! You will never change!

Wider Angle as Emiliano turns toward the Delegation.

EMILIANO: Come on———!

He walks out the door with the DELEGATION *striding behind him. . . .*

Dissolve to:
Interior, Corridor in a Semi-Ruined Hacienda

It is the corridor which leads to the great central hall or drawing room.

Exactly in the same tempo, EMILIANO *and the* DELEGATION *are striding through a corridor.*

Interior, the Central Hall

It is a mess. CAMERA PANS *around room to disclose: windows are broken; a little charcoal fire burns in the middle of a parqueted hall; a* VERY OLD INDIAN

WOMAN *is cooking; pigs and chickens wander about the room, over the Oriental rugs and upholstered chairs; in a great chair sits a blowsy, blondined* WOMAN, *slightly fat and unattractive, very drunk and asleep with her mouth open. . . .* CAMERA STOPS *on* EUFEMIO, *lying on a couch. He is up on one elbow, a wine glass in his hand. He is drunk and dangerous. Balefully he watches his* BROTHER *and the* DELEGATION *approach and stop in front of him. His hand rests lightly on the butt of a gun in his holster.* EMILIANO *stops in front of him.*

Medium Shot—Emiliano and Eufemio

EUFEMIO: Brother, be careful what you say to me!
EMILIANO: Eufemio, did you take land away from these people?
EUFEMIO: I took what I wanted.
An INDIAN WOMAN *behind* EUFEMIO *moves.*
EMILIANO: Eufemio, I . . .
EUFEMIO: I took their wives, too.
He looks directly at a MAN *who stands behind* EMILIANO.

Close Shot—the Man

We recognize him as a MEMBER *of the* DELEGATION. *He is looking at the* WOMAN *behind* EUFEMIO. *Murder is in the air.*

Close Shot—the Woman, her eyes filled with shame and fear.

Group Shot around Eufemio and Emiliano

EMILIANO *(with sudden terrific violence)*: What kind of an animal are you?
EUFEMIO *(topping him)*: Animal? I'm a man! Not a freak like my brother.
EMILIANO: Get out of here. . . .
EUFEMIO: I fought as long and as hard as you did.

103

Every day you fought, I fought. I'm a general. Here's my pay—*(turning his pocket inside out)*—a little dust. I can't buy a bottle of tequila. We beat Díaz. He's living in a palace in Paris. I've got a hut. We beat Huerta. He's a rich man in the United States. I have to beg pennies in my home village from people who never fired a gun! Well now, since I'm a general I'm going to act like a general. I'll take what I want. Let no one try and stop me. *(he turns and addresses the* WOMAN *behind him very directly)* Come on.

Close-up—the Woman

A quick glance off at her HUSBAND.

Close-up—the Husband

His eyes glued on his WIFE.

Group Shot

EUFEMIO *exits, the* WOMAN *following. When they have gone* EMILIANO *turns, looks at the* HUSBAND. *He drops his eyes.* EMILIANO *looks at the* MEN *around him. He* SPEAKS, *in an atmosphere charged with murder. He is talking about the land, but he's also referring to the* WOMAN.

EMILIANO: This land is yours. But you'll have to protect it. It won't be yours long if you don't protect it. And if necessary, with your lives. And your children with their lives. Don't discount your enemies. They'll be back. But if your house is burned, build it again. If your corn is destroyed, replant. If your children die, bear more. And if they drive us out of the valleys we will live on the sides of the mountains. But we will live. *(now he looks at the* HUSBAND *for a sentence or two)* About leaders. You've looked for leaders. For strong men without faults. There aren't any. There are only men like yourselves. They change. They desert. They die. There's no leader but yourselves.

During the last couple of sentences the HUSBAND *has moved toward the head of the passage.*

Head of Passage

The HUSBAND *is there. Coming out of the room at the end of the passage is* EUFEMIO, *loaded down with his equipment. He stands in the doorway to the room and he sees the* HUSBAND, *glares at him, then turns toward the room and* SAYS, *"Come on, Chola."*

Group Shot around Emiliano

EMILIANO: I will die, but before I do I must teach you that a strong people is the only lasting strength.

Over scene comes the SOUND *of a tremendous* OUTBREAK OF SHOOTING.

In the Hallway

EUFEMIO *and the* HUSBAND *just stand* BLASTING *away at each other. The* HUSBAND *has a shotgun. The* WOMAN *is lying on the floor between them. The* HUSBAND *keels over.*

Wider Angle—Hallway

As EMILIANO *runs in,* EUFEMIO *staggers out the door, falls outside the house.*

Exterior, House

EUFEMIO *is lying on the ground dead.* EMILIANO *comes to him. Tears fill his eyes. He is immobilized. A* MAN *comes up, stands beside him.*

MAN: They are both dead.

It is as though EMILIANO *has lost power of listening. Anyway, he knew it. More* PEOPLE *crowd around him.*

AN OFFICER *(looking down at* EUFEMIO'S *body)*: When he served the cause, he served it well.

EMILIANO *does not answer because he can't.*

ANOTHER AIDE: He was a general. What he said was

true. He fought every day we fought. We'll bury him as
a general.

EMILIANO (coming out of it, only enough to answer):
Not in the military cemetery. He didn't die in battle. I'll
take him home with me.

Dissolve to:
[*Long Shot—a Tiny Tiny Village*

> *A road goes through it. A column of* FEDERAL CAVALRY
> *suddenly rides into the village. As though on order
> they quickly dismount and go about searching the
> village.*

Closer Shot

> *The* SOLDIERS *apparently find the village completely
> deserted.*

Exterior, One of the Huts

> *A* SOLDIER *goes in to search the hut. The* C.O. *and a*
> JUNIOR OFFICER *meet in front of the hut.*

JUNIOR OFFICER: The village is deserted. There isn't a
soul here.

> *They turn toward the door of the hut as a* YELP OF
> PAIN *comes from within. The* SOLDIER *who went in to
> search now comes out, shaking his hand and grimacing
> with pain.*

THE SOLDIER: There are still coals in the ashes. *(holding
out a tortilla)* The food is still warm.

> *The* C.O. *takes the tortilla, eats it.*

C.O.: They can't be very far away.

> *A* VOICE CALLS *from offstage and they all turn.*

VOICE (offstage): We found one. . . .

Another Angle—Exterior of Hut

> TWO SOLDIERS *are holding by the elbows an* OLD,
> OLD MAN, *(*LAZARO*) and dragging him toward the
> hut. The* OLD MAN *has a crutch composed of a stick*

and a half-moonlike piece of branch. The SOLDIERS *hang onto him as though he were dangerous.*

LAZARO *(sarcastically)*: I surrender, my General. But I hate to tell you—when you've caught me, you've caught nothing.

C.O.: Where are the people? Where is Zapata?

> LAZARO, *with a vague circular gesture of the hand points to the surrounding hills vaguely. . . .*

LAZARO: Up there. . . .

C.O.: When did they go . . . ?

LAZARO: Just before you came. . . .

> *There's a tiny pause.*

LAZARO: Why don't you go up after them . . . ?

> *With a quick brutality, the* JUNIOR OFFICER *smacks the* OLD MAN *on the face and knocks him down.*

LAZARO: I remember you went up after some last week.

> *The* JUNIOR OFFICER *knocks him down again. The* OLD MAN, *with a kind of frightening smile,* SPEAKS *with almost a sense of pity. . . .*

LAZARO: My son, I'm too old to be afraid.

JUNIOR OFFICER *(to the* C.O.*)*: Your orders, sir.

C.O.: Orders? How can you fight an enemy you can't see???

LAZARO: You can't. . . .

C.O. *(coldly—he's done it many times before)*: Burn the village.

> MEN *come toward the* CAMERA *with burning torches.*

Dissolve to:]
Interior, a Government office

> *A different* GROUP OF MEN. *The leader is a* NEW GEN-ERAL. *All the* MEN *are in uniform. Among them is the* OLD GENERAL *we saw in the scene with* EMILIANO *in this room.*

NEW GENERAL: Always the same report! Always the same—

YOUNG OFFICER: Sir, how can you fight an enemy you can't see?

NEW GENERAL: You're looking for an army to fight. There is no army. Every man, woman, and child in the State of Morelos is Zapata's army. There is only one way. Wipe them out, all of them.

YOUNG OFFICER: Excuse me, sir. We can't find anybody to wipe out. We go there. The corn is growing; there is a fire in the hearth . . . and no one! We burn the house—we destroy the corn—we go back there. A new shelter! The corn is growing again. And the people—like a different race! They aren't afraid of anything!

OLD GENERAL (*with the subtlest irony . . . the faintest smile*): Gentlemen—this is not a man . . . it's an idea and it's spreading. . . .

A HARSH VOICE *breaks in:*

VOICE: It's a *man*!

Close Shot—Fernando in their uniform.

FERNANDO: It's Zapata! Cut off the head of this snake and the body will die!

Wider Angle—Fernando and Group

OLD GENERAL: Ideas are harder to kill than snakes. How do you kill an idea?

FERNANDO: Kill Zapata and your problem is solved.

[YOUNG OFFICER: But how? We surrounded his village; he was there; he got away. Then we surrounded his house; he was there; he got away.

With a contemptuous look at all of them, FERNANDO *goes to the door and opens it.*

FERNANDO: Come in, Colonel.

An unshaven, disheveled derelict of a MAN *comes through the door. . . .*

FERNANDO: Sit down, Colonel.

The DERELICT *looks around the room. His eyes are uneasy, wary, glazed. He sits.*

Two Shot—Fernando and Guajardo

FERNANDO: Have you considered my proposition?

GUAJARDO: I was a soldier . . . I have never done anything like that.

FERNANDO *(interrupting)*: Since you were a soldier, then you know that the object of war is to win.

GUAJARDO: I'll think about it. I'll answer tomorrow.

His eyes go to a bottle of liquor on the table.

FERNANDO: Answer *now*!

GUAJARDO *(his hand shakes—his eyes on the liquor)*: May I have a drink . . . ?

FERNANDO: After you decide. . . .

Wider Angle—Favoring Guajardo

GUAJARDO: If I should refuse to carry out what you— It would be dangerous because I know your plan. . . . *(pause)* I would be put in protective custody. *(pause)* It is logical that I would try to escape, and I would be killed in the attempt. In effect, I have no choice!

FERNANDO: You are very intelligent! *(to* ANOTHER MAN*)* Give the Colonel a drink.

Dissolve to:
A Stream—Indian Women Washing—Among Them Josefa

JOSEFA *is finishing. Her* FATHER'*s prediction has come true—she is practically indistinguishable from the* OTHERS. *Just now she is listening to the* WOMEN TALK-ING.

FIRST WOMAN: I heard them talking . . . they said something about new rifles. They are very happy.

SECOND WOMAN *(to* JOSEFA*)*: What is it, Josefa?

JOSEFA *(gathering up her things, preparing to go)*: What?

SECOND WOMAN: What is going on about ammunition, rifles?

A Close Shot—Josefa

She is very worried.

JOSEFA: I don't know. Emiliano doesn't tell me. . . .

Full Shot—Group of Women as Josefa leaves.

Quick Dissolve to:
Exterior, Hill—Moonlight

THREE HORSES *coming up the hill.*

Interior, Zapata's Hut

EMILIANO *and* JOSEFA *in bed. Their eyes are open, staring straight up. Over the shot the* SOUND OF RIDING.

Very Close Shot, the eyes of Emiliano and Josefa.

Medium Shot

ZAPATA *has moved down toward the end of the bed. He grabs his pants, and settles back, putting them on. As he moves back the* CAMERA PANS *to include* JOSEFA *coming toward him with his carbine. She is covered with a* rebozo, *and that's all. But it covers practically all of her. They have been sleeping naked.* SOUND OF KNOCKING *outside.*]

Another Angle

ZAPATA *takes the gun and goes toward the door. He opens it a crack, revealing the* CHARRO. *He goes outside.*

Exterior, Hut

FOUR *perspiring* MEN *waiting.* EMILIANO *comes out.*
EMILIANO: Well?
CHARRO: We saw the supplies. The guns are new. Some never fired. Machine guns, too.
EMILIANO: Ammunition?
CHARRO: A mountain of it.
The door behind them opens, and JOSEFA, *staying well screened behind the door, hands out water. The* MEN *drink as they* TALK.
EMILIANO: You saw the ammunition?
CHARRO: Yes.
EMILIANO *(thoughtfully)*: This could give us a year and in a year we'd be ready for anything.

110

Interior, Hut

JOSEFA *listening. The* VOICES *come over her.*

EMILIANO'S VOICE: Why does he want to join us?

CHARRO'S VOICE: He says he was stripped of his rank for nothing. He wants revenge.

EMILIANO'S VOICE: Stripped of his rank, and now he's suddenly a Colonel with a first-class regiment. Sounds like a trap.

CHARRO'S VOICE: Yes.

EMILIANO'S VOICE: But it's also strange enough to be true.

CHARRO'S VOICE: Yes.

Exterior, Hut

EMILIANO: How is he going to prove good faith?

CHARRO: He executed Juan Calsado, the Chief of Police who killed so many of our people. Further proof he leaves to you.

EMILIANO: Does he? Come back at sunset ready to ride. I'll think out some proofs by then. . . .

He starts into the house.

Interior, Hut

EMILIANO *comes by the door. We get a glimpse of* JOSEFA—*enough to note that she has been there all the time. The* CAMERA FOLLOWS EMILIANO, *who goes and throws himself on the bed.* JOSEFA *still stands by the door. The* HORSEMEN *can be* HEARD *going off.*

JOSEFA: What has happened?

EMILIANO: Something! Nothing!

JOSEFA: Emiliano, I want to know.

EMILIANO: What?

JOSEFA: What is happening?

EMILIANO: Are the hens beginning to crow?

JOSEFA *goes over to the bed and lies on it with* EMILIANO. *They are outside the covers. He is lying on his back. She is very tender and loving. Toward the end*

111

of the following SPEECH *she begins to make love to him, kissing him with a wild but helpless love.*

JOSEFA: Emiliano, every night I have the same thought. My heart says, now you have your husband for the first time, alone sometimes, without fighting, running, hiding. But my heart also says you will be dead soon and I have never known you in peace.

EMILIANO: Josefa, enough! I'm trying to make a plan. . . . We're getting the ammunition we need.

JOSEFA: I don't want to hear.

EMILIANO: Josefa. . . .

JOSEFA *(suddenly, full of the harshest bitterness)*: My father told me! "You'll squat over the grinding stone," he said. "You'll beat your clothes clean on a river stone. You'll walk behind him on the trail and he will only speak to give you orders." And I said, "I love him and I will have him." *(pauses)* And now you do not talk to me, and one day you will be gone and a stranger will come to the door and tell me you are dead. This is what is left for me. . . . This is what is left for me. . . .

EMILIANO, *feeling her great pain, now* SPEAKS. *With difficulty.*

EMILIANO: A Federal Colonel is giving his regiment and equipment to us.

JOSEFA: A trick?

EMILIANO: I always suspect a trick. I wouldn't be alive now, if I didn't.

JOSEFA: This is an easy way to kill you.

EMILIANO: I haven't even decided to meet with him yet.

JOSEFA: Don't go, Emiliano.

EMILIANO: We need the ammunition.

JOSEFA: I have a feeling. Don't go!

EMILIANO: That's enough now. I'll make up my mind.

JOSEFA: Emiliano. . . .

EMILIANO: Josefa, enough! I haven't decided. . . .

JOSEFA: Do you *want* to die?

EMILIANO: I must do what's needed. *(looks at her)* It will

112

be all right. If I go down, I'll buy you two new dresses, both beautiful.

But he, himself, is now troubled. He can't look at her, moves away. . . . Then turns and SAYS,

EMILIANO: I must do what's needed.

JOSEFA: I won't speak again. I won't speak again. . . .

He takes her in his arms.

Dissolve to:

[*A Field of Battle—a Tent—Fires Burning—Executions*

GUAJARDO *is pouring himself a drink. He throws it down. Now another.* CHARRO *enters.*

GUAJARDO: Well? Did you see them?

CHARRO: Yes. They are the ones who burned our home village.

GUAJARDO: Were they dead enough for you?

CHARRO: Just as dead as they deserved!

Food is brought to GUAJARDO. *He sits.*

GUAJARDO: Is he satisfied?

CHARRO: With this. Yes.

GUAJARDO: Then what?

CHARRO: He orders you to attack the garrison at Jonacatepec and to destroy it.

GUAJARDO: How large is the garrison?

CHARRO: You should know.

GUAJARDO: Of course. I'll find out. *(he can't eat)* When do I attack?

CHARRO: Now.

GUAJARDO: Tonight?

CHARRO: As soon as you can. Tonight, if you can.

He starts out.

GUAJARDO: Will this be the last test?

CHARRO *(at the door)*: After you've done it, you'll find out.

He exits. GUAJARDO *pushes the food away. Pours himself a drink.*

Dissolve:]
In Front of Emiliano and Josefa's Hut—Evening

EMILIANO *is standing, leaning against the wall. He seems to be waiting.* JOSEFA *is sitting on a low bench.*

EMILIANO: Look how the little clouds go across the face of the moon . . . the moon is racing. Time races, too. . . .

JOSEFA: It reminds me—

EMILIANO: Don't remember anything. Let your mind float. Everything is in the future.

JOSEFA *(at his feet)*: You've made up your mind. . . .

EMILIANO: Shshsh!

JOSEFA *(bitterly, in a burst)*: I don't speak for myself now. But, if anything happens to you, what would become of these people?

EMILIANO: What?

JOSEFA: What would they have left?

EMILIANO: Themselves.

JOSEFA: With all the fighting and death, what has changed?

EMILIANO: *They've* changed. That is how things really change—slowly—through people. *(with a faraway look)* They don't need me any more. (LAUGHS)

JOSEFA: They have to be led.

EMILIANO: But by each other. A strong man makes a weak people. Strong people don't need a strong man.

Wider Angle

There is a sudden entry of HORSEMEN. CHARRO *on a* HORSE *comes right up to* EMILIANO. *In the background a movement of* HORSES *continues. . . .*

Emiliano and Josefa as Charro enters to them.

EMILIANO *(to* CHARRO*)*: Well?

CHARRO: Jonacatepec is destroyed. Its garrison dead.

EMILIANO: You saw it?

CHARRO: The garrison is destroyed.

EMILIANO: The supplies?

114

CHARRO: Stacked and waiting. I saw them.

EMILIANO: What do you think?

CHARRO: He has passed every test.

EMILIANO: Then . . .

He shrugs. Looks down at JOSEFA. *She does not move.*

CHARRO: When will you go?

EMILIANO: Tonight. It's safer at night. We will leave now. *(he* CALLS*)* Otillano!

A HORSE *is brought up.* EMILIANO *looks at* JOSEFA. *She looks at him. She has never moved from her first position. Her face is full of pain. She is bitterly and completely opposed to what he is doing.*

EMILIANO: Charro—suppose something happened to me?

CHARRO: What?

EMILIANO: Someday I'll die.

CHARRO: Someday you'll die . . . and then . . . well, we wouldn't be much if— I mean, we'll get along.

EMILIANO: But look at us. They have pushed us up to the very edge of the world.

CHARRO: But we're still here. And someday we'll go down into the valleys again. Until then, we know how to survive.

EMILIANO *turns and looks at* JOSEFA. *Her face is expressionless. He smiles. She looks at him expressionless. She hasn't moved from her crouch at his feet. He mounts, turns his* HORSE, *and trots it slowly away.*

Close Shot—Josefa

Suddenly JOSEFA *is crying. Then she* SCREAMS *in terror.*

Wider Angle

EMILIANO *stops his* HORSE *and turns and rides back to her. He leans down from the saddle and cups her chin in his hand and lifts her face up.*

EMILIANO: Josefa. Don't worry, I'll be back. And this time I'll bring you two new dresses, both beautiful.

He straightens and lifts his reins. She leaps and takes hold of his bridle.

115

JOSEFA (SCREAMING): Don't go! Don't go! I beg you, Miliano, don't go! Send someone else!

The HORSE *rears in fright.* EMILIANO *has trouble controlling him.* JOSEFA *hangs on, crying hysterically. Finally* EMILIANO *leans forward and forcibly opens her hands. He wheels his* HORSE *and rides off. Other* INDIAN WOMEN *come up and comfort her.*

Dissolve to:
Long Shot—the Old Semi-Ruined Hacienda at Chinemeca

It is surrounded by a high wall. A large double gate opens into the central courtyard. Out of the gate ride FIVE MOUNTED ZAPATISTAS. *They have just completed their reconnaisance of the courtyard.* ONE *of them rides a little down the road, away from the hacienda, stands in his stirrups, and waves his hat in signal. . . .*

The Road

EMILIANO *and some* ATTENDANTS *come rapidly into sight. They ride toward us. . . . Along the edge of the road are stands of rifles, cases of ammunition, machine guns, four pieces of artillery.*

Close Shot—Emiliano

He looks admiringly at the materiel as he rides.

Full Shot

EMILIANO *rides in front of the gate and he looks into the courtyard. . . . Inside the courtyard, we can see* COLONEL GUAJARDO . . . *now cleanly dressed and in full regimentals. Behind him and at the side, stands* ZAPATA's WHITE HORSE, BLANCO, *with a beautiful new saddle and bridle.*

Close Shot—Emiliano

He has seen the HORSE. *He leaps from his* HORSE *and runs in. . . .*

116

Emiliano and Blanco

There is a love scene. The HORSE *knows him, nuzzles him.* EMILIANO *looks at* GUAJARDO.

EMILIANO: Where did you get him?

GUAJARDO: A Federal Officer had him. . . . He's yours.

EMILIANO *buries his head in the* HORSE'S *mane, rubs his forehead on the neck. . . .*

Another Angle

While ZAPATA *is occupied with the* HORSE *. . . we can see past them,* GUAJARDO *slowly, slowly backing away. . . .*

EMILIANO: Blanco! *(to* HORSE*)* Look at you! Where have you been! You've got old!

Guajardo—Foreground—Past Him We See

EMILIANO *and the* HORSE. . . . GUAJARDO *has reached a recess in the wall a few feet from* EMILIANO *and the* HORSE.

Close Shot—Emiliano and the Horse

BLANCO *suddenly raises his head* SNORTING. . . .

Guajardo

He raises his arm . . . ending in a salute.

Emiliano

He looks up and around.

The Parapets, suddenly lined with Armed Men.

Long Shot

EMILIANO *is all alone in the middle of the courtyard. . . .*

A FUSILLADE *from the parapets.*

The HORSE *rears, bolts. . . .*

Emiliano

> He has been knocked down by the very weight of the
> lead being poured into him. But he's still FIRING. . . .

Parapets

> Another VOLLEY. . . .

Close-up—Guajardo's Face

Emiliano, dying.

> Instinctively he still FIRES. Then his hand is still. . . .
> He lies there without moving. A silence. Then he
> twitches. Instantly there is another VOLLEY. . . . Now
> he is dead. . . .

Dissolve to :
Long Shot—the Courtyard Later—the Sun Is Setting

> The courtyard is empty, except for the form of ZA-
> PATA's body, covered by a serape in the center. The
> paving around the body is chipped with bullets. In the
> far background the WHITE HORSE can be seen stand-
> ing motionless. ARMED GUARDS in the shadows.

> Enter, at an opposite gate of the courtyard, FER-
> NANDO and the OLD GENERAL, attended.

> As they enter the gate, the HORSE raises his head
> and SNORTS.

> FERNANDO and the OLD GENERAL walk up to the
> body. As they walk:

OLD GENERAL: That's a beautiful horse.

FERNANDO *leans down to uncover the body.*

FERNANDO: You can have him now.

> As he throws the serape off, the HORSE first shies and
> then bolts full tilt out the gateway of the courtyard.

FERNANDO: Catch that horse. Shoot him! Shoot him!

> He seems hysterical. . . .

OLD GENERAL *(in horror)*: Shoot him. . . .

FERNANDO *(recovering and explaining not quite convincingly)*: These people are very superstitious. . . .

> *Men run out the gate. . . . *FERNANDO *and the* OLD GENERAL *look at the body.*

FERNANDO: He's dead.

OLD GENERAL: They shot him to ribbons. They must have been terribly afraid of him. *(half-hidden admiration)* The tiger is dead.

FERNANDO: And that's the end of that.

OLD GENERAL: I don't know . . . sometimes a dead man can be a terrible enemy.

> FERNANDO *stares at him a moment, comprehending. . . . Then he gets the* OLD GENERAL'S *point. . . . He explodes with real rage.*

FERNANDO: Expose his body in the plaza so they can see it! So they can *all* see that he's dead!

Dissolve to:
Long Shot—Plaza at Roma

> *About a* DOZEN HORSEMEN *of the Federal cavalry ride into the plaza. The plaza seems deserted in the brilliant sunlight. Unceremoniously,* ONE OF THE RIDERS *dumps a body on the cistern head which is the center of the plaza. Then they ride off.*

Medium Shot—Side of the Plaza

> *The figure of a* WOMAN *is seen stepping from the shadow where she cannot be identified, into the light where it is seen that she is the* SOLDADERA. *She looks much older than when we last saw her. She starts toward the body.*

Full Shot—Plaza

> *From the shadows at the sides of the plaza a number of* MEN, *young and old, cross toward the body. They do not come slowly, but quickly, lithely, like angry cats.*

121

Medium Shot Around the Body

The SOLDADERA *has composed the body. The group of* MEN *look at it curiously. An old scarred, beat-up veteran of the wars,* LAZARO, *steps up and leans down over the body. His attitude is not funereal. He has come to find out something. He examines the body for a moment, the* OTHER MEN *watching him curiously; then he turns away and spits on the ground in a gesture of contempt.*

LAZARO: Who do they think they're fooling? Shot up that way! Could be anybody!

A YOUNG MAN: He fooled them again!

ANOTHER MAN: Are you sure?

LAZARO: I rode with him. I fought with him all these years. Do they think they can fool me? They can't kill him. . . .

YOUNG MAN *(agreeing)*: They'll never get him. Can you capture a river? Can you kill the wind?

LAZARO *(violently disagreeing with* YOUNG MAN*)*: No! He's not a river and he's not the wind! He's a man—and they still can't kill him!

During this some WOMEN *have come forward, bringing flowers which they put around the body.*

A MAN *(looking around—with a sense of awe)*: Then where is he . . . ?

LAZARO: He's in the mountains. You couldn't find him now. But if we ever need him again—he'll be back.

YOUNG MAN *(with a secret kind of smile)*: Yes . . . he's in the mountains. . . .

They're all looking up. . . .

Exterior, a Mountain Slope

Over a rise of MUSIC *we see* BLANCO, *the* WHITE HORSE, *walking up the slope toward the peak. He's all alone, grazing peacefully. . . .*

Fade out

The End

STEINBECK'S SCREENPLAYS
AND PRODUCTIONS

Among modern American authors, John Steinbeck has had the greatest success with the movies, both with adaptations of his novels to the screen and as a screenwriter himself. William Faulkner supported himself for years by writing screenplays, but few of them are distinguished and all are collaborations; with a few exceptions, film versions of his own fiction have been travesties. Hemingway had power at the box office, but the movies often exploited him as if he were a pulp writer of sensational sex and violence. His only writing directly for the screen is the rather formless narrative for the documentary *The Spanish Earth*. F. Scott Fitzgerald complained that Hollywood invariably mangled any screenwriting that he was proud of.[1]

But most Steinbeck films have been both artistic and commercial successes, and a number of them have become screen classics. Steinbeck movies have received twenty-five Academy Award nominations, have won four of them, and Steinbeck himself was nominated three times for screenwriting.

Steinbeck's films fall into four categories: those adapted by others from his work, those he adapted himself from his fiction, those based upon unpublished stories that he wrote for the screen, and his original screenplays.

The best adaptations of Steinbeck novels for the movies are the first two, *Of Mice and Men* and *The Grapes of Wrath* (1940), directed respectively by Lewis Milestone and John Ford. Steinbeck had no direct hand in these productions; the screenplays by Eugene Solow and Nunnally Johnson preserved much dialogue verbatim from

[1] Cf. John Schultheiss, "The 'Eastern' Writer in Hollywood," *Cinema Journal*, 11 (Fall 1971), 13–45.

the novels but sometimes softened Steinbeck's harsh details and then-censorable language. George Bluestone and Warren French have shown how the script for *The Grapes of Wrath* blunts the novel's detailed attacks on specific oppressors and how, by rearranging sequences, it gives the film an upbeat ending that takes away the necessity for social and political action. Even so, both films created a visual and dramatic record of the Depression that is both historically valuable and transcends the period in a timeless account of man's inhumanity to man, the American loneliness, and the dream of a place of one's own. Both have become part of American folklore. Musically, *Of Mice and Men* offered a distinctive score by Aaron Copland, and *The Grapes of Wrath* prompted Woody Guthrie to write the folk song "Tom Joad."

Since Steinbeck himself was a playwright whose stage version of *Of Mice and Men* won the New York Drama Critics' Circle Award, it would seem natural for him to adapt his own work for the screen. Nowadays, writers often do so. But in the 1930s and 1940s, few novelists of note worked on films of their own books. Instead, they were usually put to hackwork on other people's projects. Therefore, despite the commercial success of *The Grapes of Wrath*, Steinbeck did not pursue Hollywood's big money.

Instead, he wrote the script for *The Forgotten Village*, a semidocumentary film about science versus superstition in a small Mexican mountain village. For this project, he teamed up with director/producer Herbert Kline, to whom he wrote, "Zanuck is offering me five thousand a week to write a Hollywood movie, but I like your offer better, Herb—to write with no pay on a film I really want to do in Mexico. . . ."[2] Steinbeck's long-standing interest in Mexico had been whetted the year before by his trip with marine biologist Edward F. Ricketts into the

[2] Herbert Kline, "On John Steinbeck," *Steinbeck Quarterly*, 4 (Summer 1971), 82–83.

Gulf of California and by their collaboration on the documentary study, *Sea of Cortez*. Now he joined Kline on location and spent months in Mexico becoming familiar with details of village life and with the efforts of the Mexican Rural Medical Service to overcome the hostility of *curanderos*, or herbalist healers, and the Indians' fatalism toward disease. Steinbeck explained that his screenplay was "a very elastic story," that was actually a question, to which he found the answers when "the crew moved into the village, made friends, talked, and listened."[3] Since the film-makers planned to use illiterate Indians who knew no English and in some cases not even Spanish, Steinbeck could not write a conventional scenario with dialogue. The villagers spoke naturally among themselves in their own language while enacting Steinbeck's story. In many cases, Kline captured the details of village life as they happened. Steinbeck's screenplay is entirely a narration, spoken by Burgess Meredith.

The Forgotten Village won numerous prizes as a feature documentary but played only in small independent art theaters because the major studios then controlled most distribution through block booking. As in *Viva Zapata!*, *The Forgotten Village* shows Steinbeck's concern for the Mexican peasants and his desire to improve their condition. His protagonist, an Indian boy named Juan Diego, is driven away from his village after he brings in doctors to fight a cholera epidemic by inoculating the children and disinfecting poisoned wells. The superstitious villagers consider inoculation to be a form of diabolism and would rather have their children die and go to heaven, but Juan Diego saves his afflicted sister. Banished, he goes to the city to become a physician and eventually return to enlighten his people. The film itself helped bring enlightenment, for a Mexican villager some years later told Kline, "Jefe, the children do not die here any more."

[3] John Steinbeck, *The Forgotten Village* (New York: The Viking Press, 1941), p. 5.

Steinbeck was not personally involved in the next two films made from his fiction. In 1942, M-G-M made a sentimentalized version of *Tortilla Flat* that was notable mainly for the performance of Frank Morgan as the Pirate, for which he received an Academy Award nomination as best supporting actor. A year later, Twentieth Century-Fox made a competent low-budget movie of *The Moon Is Down*, with a screenplay by Nunnally Johnson. Steinbeck's stage verson had only a nine-week run, so when Johnson asked Steinbeck for suggestions on the screenplay, the author replied, "Tamper with it." Johnson followed Steinbeck's plot and dialogue carefully but opened up the action and dramatized episodes that are only offstage in the novel and play. Accordingly, most reviewers found the film more effective than its source in dramatizing German brutality and the growing fury and resistance of the villagers. Steinbeck himself acknowledged, "There is no question that pictures are a better medium for this story than the stage ever was. It was impossible to bring the whole countryside and the feeling of it onto the stage, with the result that the audience saw only one side of the picture."[4]

When *The Moon Is Down* was first published as a novel, some critics and readers condemned it for being "soft" on Nazism by daring to portray the German troopers as human beings. Clearly, the novel is anti-Nazi, however, and the movie version won better acceptance; but the controversy was revived with Steinbeck's next war film. In 1944, Twentieth Century-Fox released a picture billed as "Alfred Hitchcock's Production of *Lifeboat* by John Steinbeck." Actually, the scenario is by Jo Swerling, who had written *The Westerner*, *Pride of the Yankees*, and other Gary Cooper films for Samuel Goldwyn. Steinbeck's original story is unpublished, and it is unclear how much detail was provided by himself, Swerling, and

4 "Brighter Moon," *Newsweek*, 21 (April 5, 1943), 86.

Hitchcock. Hitchcock states that he originally assigned Steinbeck to the screenplay but considered his treatment incomplete. He had MacKinlay Kantor work on it briefly but didn't like the results and he then turned the project over to Swerling. Finding the narrative still rather shapeless, he then went over it himself.[5]

The characters and dialogue are not characteristically Steinbeckian, but the form and philosophy of the film resemble some of his novels. As in *The Wayward Bus*, Steinbeck isolates a group of representative figures and lets them interact. All the action is confined to a ship's launch containing the survivors of an Allied freighter sunk by a German submarine, plus the commander of the submarine, which was also destroyed in the encounter. The lifeboat becomes a microcosm, and the film an allegory of the war, with the democratic nations adrift at sea.

The controversy arose over the contrast between the Nazi and the democratic survivors. The latter are usually divided and ineffectual, while the Nazi, with singleminded purpose, is so resourceful and confident that the others often turn to him for leadership. Hostile critics accused Steinbeck of perpetrating the myth of the Aryan superman. Actually, the Nazi is treacherous, sinister, and murderous. When the others discover how he has betrayed them, they turn on him in hysterical rage, beat him savagely, and drown him. This nautical lynching resembles the mob violence of *In Dubious Battle* and of "The Vigilante." But Steinbeck also wrote in *In Dubious Battle* that "There's a hunger in men to work together," and the democratic survivors do learn some teamwork and generally grow in sympathy and humanity.

Hitchcock interpreted Steinbeck's allegory as meaning that "while the democracies were completely disorganized,

[5] François Truffaut, *Hitchcock*, with the Collaboration of Helen G. Scott (New York: Simon and Schuster, 1967), p. 113.

all of the Germans were clearly headed in the same direction. So here was a statement telling the democracies to put their differences aside temporarily and to gather their forces to concentrate on the common enemy, whose strength was precisely derived from a spirit of unity and of determination."[6]

Expertly directed by Hitchcock, with oustanding performances by Tallulah Bankhead, William Bendix, and Walter Slezak, *Lifeboat* was a popular success. *Time* found it "remarkably intelligent" and called it "an adroit allegory of world shipwreck."[7] Other reviewers considered it thoughtful and exciting. Steinbeck received an Academy Award nomination for the best original story. But other reviewers complained that the realism was actually bland and superficial, and James Agee judged the allegory clever but contrived.

For Steinbeck studies, *Lifeboat* is notable for its use of allegory (as in *The Grapes of Wrath*, *The Wayward Bus*, and *East of Eden*) and for such recurring Steinbeck themes as group man, the stripping away of civilized surfaces, the brutality of people carried away by mass violence, and the nature of leadership. The finished film is more an ingenious entertainment than a serious study of these themes, but it is unclear how much of the slick surface was Steinbeck's and how much was veneer provided by Swerling and Hitchcock. At any rate, *Lifeboat* is a thoroughly professional piece of moviemaking and it shows that Steinbeck was learning to write more than documentary narrative for the films.

Steinbeck was not yet ready to undertake an entire screenplay, however. His third World War II movie, *A Medal for Benny*, has a screenplay by Frank Butler, based on an unpublished story by Steinbeck and Jack Wagner. The screenplay has been published in *Best Film Plays*,

[6] *Ibid.*
[7] *Time*, 43 (January 31, 1944), 94.

1945, edited by John Gassner and Dudley Nichols. Benny, the title character, is a brawling *paisano* like Danny and Pilon in *Tortilla Flat*. He never appears in the picture, for the police have run him out of his small California town, and he has joined the Army. The girl he left behind him, Lolita Sierra (Dorothy Lamour), is wooed in his absence by a likable ne'er-do-well, Joe Morales (Arturo De Cordova), who is certain that he is a better man than the legendary Benny. Benny is, in fact, a heel whom Lolita never really loved. But just as she agrees to marry Joe, the message comes that Benny has been killed in action and is to receive a posthumous Congressional Medal of Honor. Ignorant of Lolita's true feelings, the community expect her to spend the rest of her life in heartbroken bereavement as a tribute to the hero.

The town officials meanwhile plan to exploit the awarding of the medal for its full publicity and profit. When they realize that Benny is a Chicano from the wrong side of the tracks, they move his father temporarily from his shack into a new house in order to impress the celebrities at the ceremony. But when Charley Martini, the father, realizes how he is being used, he returns home in disgust, and the medal is awarded among the scruffy children, scratching chickens, and careless surroundings of his old neighborhood. The hitherto comic Charley now takes on dignity as he asserts that a hero can come from any kind of background and not just from the Establishment. At the end, Joe goes off to war, but it is now clear that Lolita is his girl and will be waiting for him.

A Medal for Benny succeeds admirably on its modest terms and was considered one of the best films of 1945. J. Carrol Naish was nominated for the Academy Award as best supporting actor for his performance as Charley, and Steinbeck and Jack Wagner received nominations for the best original story. Bosley Crowther wrote that "Particular credit is here given to Mr. Steinbeck because the spirit of the work is so richly consistent with the spirit of all his *'paisano'* yarns."[8]

Steinbeck was now ready to undertake a full screenplay, though not yet completely on his own. His next film was an adaptation of his novella *The Pearl*. This parable of a poor Mexican fisherman who learns that wealth brings corruption and death was not promising material for Hollywood. Steinbeck teamed up with a Mexican company to make the film in Mexico with Mexican performers acting in English. Released by RKO in 1948, *The Pearl* was the first Mexican movie to be widely distributed in the United States.

Steinbeck wrote the screenplay in collaboration with director Emilio Fernandez and Jack Wagner, co-author of the story *A Medal for Benny*. The adaptation is faithful to Steinbeck's plot but alters some significant details. In a comparison of the film and the book, Charles R. Metzger notes that Kino's brother Juan Tomás and the priest are omitted, the great machete with which Kino defends himself is left out, and a drinking sequence and an extravagant fiesta are added. Metzger argues that these changes weaken the novella's symbolism and diffuse its themes, but he concludes that the film still retains most of Steinbeck's *exemplum* of corruption and survival.[9] The main liabilities of the production were that the leads were too glamorous, the supporting players came out of central casting, and the costumes out of a well-laundered studio wardrobe. *The Pearl* lacks the authentic poverty and weather-worn faces of *The Forgotten Village*, but this is the fault of the director, not of Steinbeck. To compensate, *The Pearl* has superb photography of Baja California seascapes and beautifully composed shots that John McCarten compared to the murals of Orozco, who had also

[8] Bosley Crowther, "Review of *A Medal for Benny*," *The New York Times*, May 24, 1945, p. 15:2.

[9] Charles R. Metzger, "The Film Version of Steinbeck's *'The Pearl'*," *Steinbeck Quarterly*, 4 (Summer 1971), 88–92.

illustrated the book. In its picture of Mexican peasant life and its attacks on the exploitation of the poor by the unjustly wealthy, *The Pearl* has affinities with *Viva Zapata!*

Steinbeck, in fact, began his research on Zapata at that time. Meanwhile, he wrote a screenplay for Republic's 1949 production of *The Red Pony*. Consisting of four loosely connected short stories, *The Red Pony* lacks a strong central narrative. However, there had been a number of successful movies in the 1940s featuring a child and an animal—the *Lassie* series, *My Friend Flicka*, *National Velvet*, and *The Yearling*—and Republic seemed to think that *The Red Pony* could repeat the formula. But Steinbeck's episodes lack sentimental appeal. Essentially grim, they focus on Jody Tiflin's painful initiation into an understanding of suffering, death, and the difficulties of adulthood, with a psychological and biological realism that is far from the usual Hollywood pastoral romance.

Blending these stories into a commercially popular picture was a considerable challenge. Steinbeck wrote the screenplay himself, the only time he had the sole responsibility for adapting one of his books. Combining "The Gift," "The Leader of the People," and part of "The Promise," in that order, with a more affirmative ending, Steinbeck produced a loose, leisurely narrative that some reviewers found unexciting. Perhaps because the boy in M-G-M's 1946 movie of *The Yearling* is also named Jody, Steinbeck changed Jody Tiflin's name to Tom. For no particular reason, he altered the parents' names from Carl and Ruth Tiflin to Fred and Alice. Considering the problems of adaptation, the screenplay is quite competent. Lewis Milestone, who had made *Of Mice and Men*, did a routine job of direction with somewhat miscast players (Myrna Loy as the mother, Shepperd Strudwick as the father, Louis Calhern as the grandfather, young Robert Mitchum as Billy Buck, and Peter Miles as the boy). In the long run, the most memorable feature of the film has been the vigorous score by Aaron Copland.

Steinbeck's only completely original screenplay with dialogue is *Viva Zapata!*, unquestionably his finest work in the genre. Elia Kazan says that the initial idea for a film on Zapata was his. "I went to John who lived a few doors down the block. We were extremely close friends. I asked him if he'd be interested in working on it with me. He said he'd been thinking about Z for years."[10] In fact, according to Richard Astro, Steinbeck first became interested in Zapata around 1930, from talking in Los Angeles to Reina Dunn, the daughter of H. H. Dunn, a Hearst journalist who later wrote a meretricious book about Zapata entitled *The Crimson Jester, Zapata of Mexico*.[11] Dunn's book, published in 1934, perpetrated the yellow journalism of anti-Zapata newspapers such as the *Imparcial*, which called Zapata "the modern Attila" and described his rebels as bandits who raped and ransacked in an orgy of violence. Steinbeck read this book but rejected its sensationalism; his own research for the film provided quite a different portrait of a restrained and responsible leader. What particularly intrigued him, according to Kazan, was "Z's giving up power when he had it, the fact that he found it corrupting and he went back to Morelos."[12]

Steinbeck's research in Mexico for *The Forgotten Village* reinforced his interest in the themes of *Viva Zapata!* For *The Forgotten Village*, he joined forces with director Herbert Kline and cinematographer Alexander Hackensmid (now known as Hammid), who had made two anti-Fascist documentaries, *Lights Out in Europe* and *Crisis*. Together, the three of them had planned to film a documentary about the attempt by Fascists in Mexico to overthrow the liberal government of President Lázaro Cardenas. While Kline and his assistants were scouting out

[10] Elia Kazan, Letter to Robert E. Morsberger, March 29, 1973.

[11] Richard Astro, Letter to Morsberger, September 29, 1971.

[12] Kazan to Morsberger, March 29, 1973.

132

locations, Steinbeck wrote a draft for such a story; but when he joined the crew in Mexico, he became more interested in the material Kline had found about the frustrated efforts of rural doctors to combat diseases and superstition among the Indian villagers, and this became the new subject of the script.[13] During production, wealthy landowners protested the peasants' being paid fair wages and tried to sabotage the production. From the research and location filming, Steinbeck acquired a first-hand knowledge of the peasant farmers; and despite his attack on their superstitious hostility to modern medicine, he developed a respect and affection for them. In addition, his experience with reactionary landowners, his meeting with progressive President Cardenas, and his initial concept of a film about civil war between Fascists and liberals helped lay the groundwork for *Viva Zapata!* a decade later.

Herbert Kline recalls that during their work on *The Forgotten Village*, he, Steinbeck, and others made a trip to Chalco, "in the heart of what was Zapataland during the Revolution. The village square was filled this day which was devoted to remembrance of Zapata. We stopped in a *pulquería* and spoke to some of the slightly to very filled with pulque, mescal, tequila locals . . . who spoke of the legend of Zapata still being alive in the mountains nearby, riding his horse . . , and looking after the peons he came from and loved." Kline suggests further that the atmosphere of Chalco that day, with "plastered and laughing" villagers playing matador with "calf-sized *toros*," provided some of the environment of *Viva Zapata!*[14]

When he undertook the screenplay for Kazan, Steinbeck did extensive research on Zapata and the Mexican revolution. His chief literary source was *Zapata the Unconquerable* (1941), a novelized biography by Edgcumb Pinchon, which was the latest book in English on the

[13] Kline, "On John Steinbeck," *loc. cit.*
[14] Kline, Letter to Morsberger, June 5, 1973.

subject until the definitive treatment by John Womack, Jr., in 1969. Womack notes that Pinchon spent a year researching in Mexico and "produced a good popular biography."[15] Pinchon's book provided only the historical outline for the screenplay. In fact Steinbeck omits most of Pinchon's material and parallels only a few scenes (the audience with Díaz, Pablo's return from Texas, the procession with Zapata as prisoner, the audience with Madero, and a conversation between Zapata and Villa), all of which he makes more incisively dramatic. More significant is what Steinbeck adds—the role of brother Eufemio (barely mentioned by Pinchon); Zapata's courtship and marriage to Josefa; the killing of Pablo; the death of Eufemio; Zapata's abdication of power; the entire role of Fernando; and most of the political philosophy.

More important than Pinchon's book was the research Steinbeck did on location in Mexico, interviewing old Zapatistas and other survivors of the revolution and getting the feel of people and places. This is what makes *Viva Zapata!* an authentically moving drama, unlike the stilted textbook or sentimentally melodramatic film biographies that Hollywood produced in the 1930s and 1940s of Clive of India, Ferdinand de Lesseps, Stephen Foster, Woodrow Wilson, the House of Rothschild, and a gallery of artists, composers, and inventors.

The Mexican revolution was so complex that it would be impossible for any film to reproduce it in close detail— even in a production as long as *Nicholas and Alexandra*. Steinbeck made no effort to do so. The structure of *Viva Zapata!* is like Shakespeare's chronicle histories, episodic yet tightly coherent, with a few skirmishes to sketch in an entire war. His screenplay is not so much history as folklore, parable, and poetry. He intended parts of it to be unspoken and accompanied by traditional Mexican

[15] John Womack, Jr., *Zapata and the Mexican Revolution* (New York: Alfred A. Knopf, 1969), p. 422.

songs called *corridos*, in this case to "be written by a wandering poet named John Steinbeck to music by Alex North" and performed by one of Zapata's men, or else "to be accompanied by either guitar music solo or music from our conception of a typical five-piece Mexican Country band."[16] Like a ballad, Steinbeck's script simplifies from diverse sources to get a more direct impact.

The actual events in the film covered a period of ten years, from 1909 to 1919. Though Steinbeck's Zapatistas speak of long and arduous campaigning, there is no sense of such a long period, and none of the film's characters age perceptibly. The oppression of the Morelos peasant farmers by the deliberate action of a plutocracy of planters resembles *The Grapes of Wrath*; but instead of providing historical detail on social and economic conditions, Steinbeck brings them to life with a few incisive scenes—an audience with Díaz, soldiers gunning down peasants trying to establish boundaries, the murder of Innocente, and the arrest of Zapata. The exposition is dramatic rather than documentary; the actors and the audience are involved more than they are informed. In the film, we never learn of the background of Madero as a schoolteacher who campaigned for president against Díaz; we first hear of him via Fernando, when Madero is already in exile in Texas. But Steinbeck's portrait of him matches Womack's account of Madero's "characteristic innocence . . . touching gentleness, concern, and sincerity."[17]

In the film, Zapata's patron, Don Nacio de la Torre, gets him pardoned for his early acts of rebellion. In actuality, Ignacio de la Torre y Mier was Díaz's son-in-law; instead of getting Zapata pardoned, he got him discharged from the Army, into which he had been drafted in 1910; in return, Zapata worked "as chief groom in his Mexico

16 Steinbeck, "Note to the Reader," Twentieth Century-Fox, July 31, 1950.
17 Womack, p. 57.

City stables."[18] Later, again in active opposition to Díaz, Zapata sent Pablo Torres Burgos to Texas to discover if Madero was sincere. But this Pablo, who became a Zapatista commander, otherwise had nothing in common with the peasant Pablo Gómez of the film; and Zapata never killed him or any other Pablo. The entire relationship is Steinbeck's fiction.

After Díaz abdicated and sailed to Paris in May 1911, Zapata demanded agrarian reform, and Madero stalled, as in the film; but the movie considerably oversimplifies Huerta's treachery during the disarming of Morelos. In fact there were several episodes when the Zapatistas began to disarm, were betrayed, and fought back. When Huerta invaded Morelos in August 1911, it was with Madero's backing. But two episodes in the film at this point correspond to the facts in detail. On one occasion, Zapata did use Madero's watch to argue against disarming, insisting, "Look, Señor Madero, if I take advantage of the fact that I'm armed and take away your watch and keep it, and after a while we meet, both of us armed the same, would you have a right to demand that I give it back?" "Certainly," said Madero. "Well," argued Zapata, "that's exactly what has happened to us in Morelos, where a few planters have taken over by force the villages' lands. My soldiers—the armed farmers and all the people in the villages—demand that I tell you, with full respect, that they want the restitution of their lands to be got under way right now."[19] Madero then promised to visit Morelos and inspect conditions there himself.

Likewise, as in the film, Eufemio wanted to shoot Madero when Huerta's troops began movements while Zapata was again disbanding his men. Madero insisted there was a misunderstanding. In the film, Madero is sincere, but in fact he kept betraying Zapata, had his gov-

[18] *Ibid.*, p. 60.
[19] *Ibid.*, p. 96.

ernment outlaw him, and sent Huerta to capture him. By then, José María Lozano, in Congress, said, "Emiliano Zapata is no longer a man, he is a symbol. He could turn himself in tomorrow . . . but the rabble [following him] . . . would not surrender."[20]

Madero became President of Mexico in 1911 and was murdered in 1913; Huerta fled in July 1914. There were five more years until Zapata's death, but this period is greatly condensed in the film, which never attempts to explain Carranza and Obregón. In part, this condensation may be due to Steinbeck's use of Pinchon as a source, for Pinchon spent 306 of his 332 pages getting to Zapata's and Villa's meeting in 1914.

Steinbeck's screenplay omits many historic characters and instead stresses fictitious ones like Fernando, Pablo Gómez, Lazaro, the Soldadera, and the Charro whose actions re-enact Zapata's. However, Josefa is not only real, but Steinbeck's research discovered her, and the film made his marriage public for the first time.[21] John Womack writes that the film-makers "included in their simplification some factual details that complicated the superhumanly heroic image of Zapata that then prevailed—like his marriage to the daughter of a hostile local rancher, his difficulties with her, etc.—details which were then practically unknown; in introducing them, they made the character much more true to life and interesting."[22] In August 1911, Zapata married Josefa Espejo, the daughter of an Ayala livestock dealer who had died in 1909. Zapata had been courting her since before the revolution, so possibly her father had earlier opposed the match, but the film keeps him alive after the marriage, to complain about his son-in-law's failure to secure power and wealth. The film omits the fact that Josefa

20 *Ibid.*, p. 123.
21 *Ibid.*, p. 420.
22 Womack, Letter to Morsberger, April 28, 1973.

bore two children who died in infancy, and it makes no mention of Zapata's bastards, some of them born after his marriage. The shooting final ambiguously includes a camp follower named Juana, who adores Zapata; this role, however, is cut from the final film.

Though the movie alters some details of Zapata's death, it is dramatically true. The suspicions of Zapata's lieutenants, Josefa's forebodings and despair, create a sense of fated inevitability, so that the audience feel as if Zapata is riding into martyrdom. The historic Zapata was murdered on April 10, 1919, betrayed by Jesús Guajardo. The fact that the Judas in the case is named Jesus adds a macabre irony to the film. In fact, Guajardo had given Zapata a sorrel horse the day before. On it, Zapata entered the hacienda with ten followers, three of whom were killed with him. The film achieves greater tension by having Zapata alone, reunited with his lost white stallion. During this sequence, there is utter silence except for the nervous sounds of the horse, while the camera focuses recurringly on three old men withered like mummies, waiting, and on four old women in black telling their beads with the shadow of a cross on the wall. Then, as in the ending of *Butch Cassidy and the Sundance Kid* seventeen years later, we see the killing from the rooftops, filled with soldiers who cut down Zapata with a rain of bullets. Afterward, in both film and fact, Guajardo had Zapata's body dumped on the pavement of the main plaza of Cuautla. John Womack's account of the aftermath closely parallels Steinbeck's ending: "Many would not believe Zapata was dead. Odd stories began to circulate. One went that Zapata was too smart for the trap, and had dispatched a subordinate who resembled him to the fatal meeting. Anyway, it went on, the corpse on display was not Zapata's. . . . In a few days the Chief would reappear as always. Then stranger reports were passed on. The horse he rode the day he died, the sorrel Guajardo had given him—it had been seen galloping riderless through the hills. People who saw it said it was white now, white as a star. And someone thought he had glimpsed Zapata himself on it, heading hard into the Guerrero mountains to the south."[23]

Some simplification of Zapata and the Mexican revolution was inevitable. Certainly, Steinbeck's treatment is as historically and dramatically legitimate as Robert Bolt's for the Academy-Award-winning *Lawrence of Arabia*. In *Zapata and the Mexican Revolution*, John Womack calls *Viva Zapata!* "a distinguished achievement." He notes that "In telescoping the whole revolution into one dramatic episode, the movie distorts certain events and characters, some grossly; but it quickly and vividly develops a portrayal of Zapata, the villagers, and the nature of their relations and movement that I find still subtle, powerful, and true."[24] Womack thinks that the indefensible exaggerations "are the presentation of Zapata as illiterate, which he was not, and the presentation of his brother as a lush, which he was not." (However, Womack does record that Eufemio became notorious for alcoholic excesses just before his death.) Womack also challenges the role of Fernando, observing that "intellectuals had very little part in determining Zapatista policy, or in determining anything about the Mexican revolution as a whole. Most of them despaired of the revolution and left for other parts, or did what their *jefes* told them." But Fernando is not especially intellectual; like the lieutenant in Graham Greene's *The Power and the Glory*, his role is that of the ruthless revolutionary determined to destroy all opposition. "Still," concludes Womack, "what rings longest in my mind from the movie is Zapata's integrity, his suspicion of all outsiders, his absolute sense of responsibility to his local people, a sense which I think Brando captured precisely."[25]

[23] Womack, *Zapata*, p. 330.
[24] *Ibid.*, p. 420.
[25] Womack, letter to Morsberger, April 28, 1973.

The part of Zapata was not written with Brando in mind, nor were any of the roles conceived for particular players. Zanuck did not want Brando for the lead, but Kazan (who had directed him on stage and screen in *A Streetcar Named Desire*) did, and Steinbeck backed him up. Much of the artistic success of *Viva Zapata!* goes to Kazan. Though the screenplay is the essential framework, without which there is no drama, screenplays alone are comparatively stark. A stage play depends more exclusively on dialogue and therefore seems more complete to the reader, whereas a movie may convey much of its impact through wordless action, visual details, and musical effects. In this sense, *Viva Zapata!* may be the most cinematic of all Kazan's films. Previously he had distinguished himself as a director of stage plays (*Death of a Salesman*) and of their screen versions (*A Streetcar Named Desire*). Earlier films like *Boomerang!* and *Gentleman's Agreement* had relied more on character and dialogue than on action. But in *Viva Zapata!*, Kazan made full use of the movie medium to reinforce Steinbeck's ideas and symbols. The action sequences are brisk and graphic. The settings (location shooting in Roma, Texas, and other sets constructed in California at the Fox Studios or on the Fox Ranch) convey authentic local color; and Joe MacDonald's photography brings out the beauty, alternately austere and ornate, of the Mexican villages, palaces, and countryside. One of the most moving sequences in the film—the procession of villagers and farmers who free Zapata from the Rurales—is entirely a combination of visual composition and music. Alex North's score is integral; instead of drenching the film with the usual overblown symphonic score of the 1950s, North had much of his music function as a natural part of the action—as religious chants, mariachi bands, serenades, military parades—all in indigenous Mexican modes. Kazan also got the most out of his cast. The main shortcoming of the performances is the mixture of accents. Brando, Quinn, and some others undertook Mexican accents, while others portrayed Mexicans with a flat middle-American speech. Most of the supporting players were relatively little known, but all are impressive. Madero, Huerta, and Villa in the film look exactly like photographs of their historic counterparts.

Viva Zapata! was nominated for numerous Academy Awards for 1952, but won only the award for Best Supporting Actor (Quinn). Brando competed for best actor but lost to Gary Cooper in *High Noon*. Steinbeck personally received nominations for story and screenplay, but the award went to *The Lavender Hill Mob*. Alex North's musical score lost to Dimitri Tiomkin's for *High Noon*. For black-and-white art and set decoration, *Viva Zapata!* was beaten by *The Bad and the Beautiful*.

Despite the film's recognition, Steinbeck felt that it had not been adequately promoted or properly appreciated. On March 1, 1963, he wrote to Kazan proposing that they try to get *Viva Zapata!* rereleased with better studio support so that it might find a fuller audience. He argued that "The film never got off the ground" in the United States because "the studio was scared of it—at least unsure and that communicated." Steinbeck claimed that Communist pressure kept the picture from being allowed any scope in Mexico and South America and that for the same reason, "It was never shown in Russia or the satellites." The film never mentions communism, and it is never specified that Fernando is a Communist; nevertheless, the thesis that relentless totalitarians betray revolution into dictatorship was too close to communism for comfort. In fact, in 1963, Steinbeck suggested that he and Kazan could rework the film to "point up the parallel with Cuba." On the other hand, "In Europe, where people knew about revolutions, there were not these problems." Even since *In Dubious Battle*, the Communists joined with the radical right in denouncing Steinbeck; and Kazan noted that "at the end of his life they were calling him a 'jackal' and a 'running dog' and all those other absurd epithets they use."[26]

In addition, Steinbeck suggested to Kazan that the film "spread too far—tried to take in too much. It became more biography than the story of a revolt. It was obscure in time and purpose. It needed clarification." He therefore proposed reworking the picture by doing some cutting, editing, and tightening (but suggested no particular details) and by adding a commentary. No reshooting would be required. "I would like to write the commentary and perhaps read it," he said. "It's not that I would do it well but that I would do it better than anyone else because I know best what it wants to say." Steinbeck wished the title for the reissue to be changed "to the one I wanted from the beginning, *Zapata Vive*." He argued that the film came out ahead of its time and that in the early 1960s the theme "that revolutions get taken over by the wrong people after they are accomplished" might find more responsive audiences: "We would sharpen and clarify the tendency of the revolt to go Fascist as it has all over the world." With proper State Department support, possible sponsorship by the USIA, and perhaps even the backing of President Kennedy, "It would be a public service." Steinbeck proposed that he and Kazan "should ask, not for money but for participation."

Considering the conduct of foreign affairs since 1964 and our active warfare in Southeast Asia, Steinbeck's proposals seem overly optimistic, but that is a hindsight not so obvious in 1963. Kazan concurs that he and Steinbeck did try to persuade Spyros Skouras at Fox into reworking and releasing the film, but the studio refused to spend any more money on it. Probably this is just as well. *Viva Zapata!* succeeds better through dramatic action than didacticism, and a propagandistic commentary might destroy the film's lyricism and reduce it to a semi-

[26] Kazan, letter to Morsberger, August 7, 1973.

documentary. Eventually, it has found its audience, in rerelease at individual theaters and in frequent showing on television. Recently, Films Incorporated has been promoting *Viva Zapata!* as one of its first twelve films excerpted for the study of film technique in colleges and universities.

Kazan and Steinbeck were particularly committed to *Viva Zapata!* Kazan writes that he is fond and proud of it and that he thinks the title role "was the most difficult job Brando ever attempted and one of his most subtle portraits."[27]

He and Steinbeck were so pleased with their collaboration that "We were eager to do another film after this one. I suggested we do the last ninety odd pages of *East of Eden* and John gave me the boom."[28] Since Steinbeck was writing another book then, Kazan suggested that Paul Osborn do the screenplay, and Steinbeck agreed. Osborn, a playwright who wrote *Morning's at Seven* and adapted *A Bell for Adano* and *Point of No Return* for the stage, used only the final section, beginning at approximately Chapter 37 in Part Four of the novel. Eliminating the Chinese philosopher servant Lee, Osborn expanded the conflict between Cal and Aron Trask for Aron's girl Abra and for the affection of their father, Adam. The film's Cal is a more brooding, violent, and self-destructive young man than Steinbeck's character; and as played by James Dean, he became the symbol of rejected and rebellious youth. (Kazan had wanted Brando for the role, but the star was unavailable.) After Dean's death in a sports car accident, *East of Eden* became a part of the James Dean cult that generated a chapter in John Dos Passos's *Midcentury*.

The team of Steinbeck and Kazan had a considerable success, both critically and financially, with *East of*

[27] Kazan, letter to Morsberger, March 29, 1973.
[28] *Ibid.*

Eden. Kazan received an Academy Award nomination for best director, Paul Osborn for his screenplay, James Dean for best actor, and Jo Van Fleet (who won) for best supporting actress.

Two years later, Twentieth Century-Fox brought out a routine movie of *The Wayward Bus*, as a vehicle for Jayne Mansfield. William Saroyan did an initial script that followed the book carefully, but his screenplay was rejected in favor of a slick adaptation by Ivan Moffat that glamorized the characters and simplified the story. Some reviewers blamed Steinbeck for weaknesses that are in the film version but not the novel. It was the last commercial Steinbeck film.

But it was not the last film, for Barnaby Conrad wrote and produced a feature-length picture of *Flight*, expanded from the short story in *The Long Valley*. The low-budget amateur production has considerable verisimilitude and was well received in London and at the Edinburgh Film Festival but was never released commercially. Steinbeck liked the picture and proposed that Conrad add an introductory narration written and spoken by Steinbeck. Conrad did so and this introduction is Steinbeck's final writing for the movies.

STEINBECK'S FILMS

Here is a complete list of films written by John Steinbeck for the screen or adapted by Steinbeck and others from his fiction. It also includes the one film narrated by Steinbeck. The films are listed in chronological order, with the major credits.

Of Mice and Men

Screenplay by Eugene Solow, adapted from the John Steinbeck play. Directed and produced by Lewis Milestone. Musical score by Aaron Copland. A Hal Roach presentation. United Artists, 1940.

George	*Burgess Meredith*	Candy	*Roman Bohnen*
Lennie	*Lon Chaney, Jr.*	Whit	*Noah Berry, Jr.*
Mae	*Betty Field*	Jackson	*Oscar O'Shea*
Slim	*Charles Bickford*	Carlson	*Granville Bates*
Curley	*Bob Steele*	Crooks	*Leigh Whipper*

The Grapes of Wrath

Screenplay by Nunnally Johnson, adapted from the novel by John Steinbeck. Musical score by Alfred Newman. Directed by John Ford. Photography by Gregg Toland. Produced by Darryl F. Zanuck. Twentieth Century-Fox, 1940.

Tom Joad	*Henry Fonda*	Al	*O. Z. Whitehead*
Ma Joad	*Jane Darwell*	Muley	*John Qualen*
Casy	*John Carradine*	Noah	*Frank Sully*
Grampa	*Charley Grapewin*	Uncle John	*Frank Darien*
Rosasharn	*Dorris Bowdon*	Winfield	*Darryl Hickman*
Pa Joad	*Russell Simpson*	Ruth Joad	*Shirley Mills*

The Forgotten Village

Story and screenplay by John Steinbeck. Music by Hanns Eisler. Photography by Alexander Hackensmid. Narrated by Burgess Meredith. Produced and directed by Herbert Kline. An Arthur Mayer–Joseph Burstyn release, 1941.

Tortilla Flat

Screenplay by John Lee Mahin and Benjamin Glazer, based on the novel by John Steinbeck. Directed by Victor Fleming. Produced by Sam Zimbalist. M-G-M, 1942.

Pilon   *Spencer Tracy*
Danny   *John Garfield*
Dolores (Sweets) Ramirez
   Hedy Lamarr

The Pirate   *Frank Morgan*
Pablo   *Akim Tamiroff*

The Moon Is Down

Screenplay by Nunnally Johnson, based on the novel by John Steinbeck. Directed by Irving Pichel. Produced by Nunnally Johnson. Twentieth Century-Fox, 1943.

Colonel Lanser   *Sir Cedric
   Hardwicke*
Mayor Orden   *Henry Travers*
Dr. Winter   *Lee J. Cobb*
Molly Morden   *Dorris Bowdon*

Madame Orden   *Margaret
   Wycherly*
Lt. Tonder   *Peter Van Eyck*
Peder   *Irving Pichel*
George Corell   *E. J. Ballantine*

Lifeboat

Screenplay by Jo Swerling, from a story by John Steinbeck. Directed by Alfred Hitchcock. Produced by Kenneth Macgowan. Twentieth Century-Fox, 1944.

Connie Porter   *Tallulah
   Bankhead*
Gus   *William Bendix*
The German   *Walter Slezak*
Alice Mackenzie   *Mary
   Anderson*

Rittenhouse   *Henry Hull*
Kovac   *John Hodiak*
Stanley Garrett   *Hume Cronyn*
Joe   *Canada Lee*

A Medal for Benny

Screenplay by Frank Butler, from a story by John Steinbeck and Jack Wagner. Directed by Irving Pichel. Produced by Paul Jones. Paramount, 1945.

Lolita Sierra   *Dorothy Lamour*
Joe Morales   *Arturo De
   Cordova*

Charley Martini   *J. Carrol
   Naish*
Raphael Catalina   *Mikhail
   Rasummy*

The Pearl

Screenplay by John Steinbeck, Emilio Fernandez, and Jack Wagner. Directed by Emilio Fernandez. Produced by Oscar Danugers. RKO, 1948.

Kino   *Pedro Armendariz*
Juana   *Maria Elena Marques*

The Red Pony

Screenplay by John Steinbeck. Music by Aaron Copland. Directed and produced by Lewis Milestone. Republic, 1949.

Alice Tiflin *Myrna Loy*
Billy Buck *Robert Mitchum*
Grandfather *Louis Calhern*
Fred Tiflin *Shepperd Strudwick*
Tom [Jody] *Peter Miles*
Teacher *Margaret Hamilton*
Beau *Beau Bridges*

Viva Zapata!

Screenplay by John Steinbeck. Directed by Elia Kazan. Produced by Darryl F. Zanuck. Twentieth Century-Fox, 1952.

Emiliano Zapata *Marlon Brando*
Josefa *Jean Peters*
Eufemio *Anthony Quinn*
Fernando *Joseph Wiseman*
Don Nacio *Arnold Moss*
Soldadera *Margo*
Pancho Villa *Alan Reed*
Madero *Harold Gordon*
Pablo *Lou Gilbert*
Señora Espejo *Mildred Dunnock*
Huerta *Frank Silvera*

O. Henry's Full House, based on five stories: "The Cop and the Anthem," "The Clarion Call," "The Last Leaf," "The Gift of the Magi," "The Ransom of Red Chief." Narrated by John Steinbeck. Twentieth Century-Fox, 1952.

East of Eden

Screenplay by Paul Osborn, based on the novel by John Steinbeck. Music by Victor Young. Directed by Elia Kazan. Warners, 1955.

Abra *Julie Harris*
Cal Trask *James Dean*
Adam Trask *Raymond Massey*
Aron Trask *Richard Davalos*
Kate *Jo Van Fleet*
Sam *Burl Ives*
Will *Albert Dekker*
Ann *Lois Smith*

The Wayward Bus

Screenplay by Ivan Moffat, based on the novel by John Steinbeck. Produced by Charles Brackett. Twentieth Century-Fox, 1957.

Johnny Chicoy *Rick Jason*
Alice Chicoy *Joan Collins*
Camille *Jayne Mansfield*
Ernest Horton *Dan Dailey*
Norma *Betty Lou Keim*
Mildred Pritchard *Dolores Michaels*
Pritchard *Larry Keating*
Morse *Robert Bray*
Mrs. Pritchard *Kathryn Givney*

Flight

Screenplay by Barnaby Conrad, adapted from the short story by John Steinbeck. Produced by Barnaby Conrad. Music written and played by Laurindo Almeida. Directed by Louis Bispo.

BIBLIOGRAPHY

Bluestone, George. *Novels into Film*. Baltimore: Johns Hopkins Press, 1957; Berkeley and Los Angeles: University of California Press, 1966. Includes a detailed study of the film version of *The Grapes of Wrath*.

Bogdanovich, Peter. *John Ford*. Berkeley: University of California Press, 1968. Contains a discussion with the director about the film of *The Grapes of Wrath*.

Camus, Albert. *The Rebel*, trans. Anthony Bower. New York: Alfred A. Knopf, Vintage Books, 1957. The classic study of rebellion and revolution.

————. *Resistance, Rebellion, and Death*, trans. Justin O'Brien. New York: Alfred A. Knopf, 1961.

Carpenter, Frederic I. "The Philosophical Joads," *College English*, II (January 1941).

Ciment, Michel. *Kazan on Kazan*. New York: The Viking Press, 1974.

Crowther, Bosley. "Review of 'A Medal for Benny,'" *The New York Times* (May 24, 1945), 15:2.

Everson, William K. *The Films of Hal Roach*. Greenwich, Connecticut: Museum of Modern Art, New York, 1971. Discusses the filming of *Of Mice and Men*.

French, Warren. *Filmguide to The Grapes of Wrath*. Bloomington: Indiana University Press, 1973.

Gassner, John, and Nichols, Dudley, eds. *Best Film Plays, 1945*. New York: Crown, 1947. Contains Frank Butler's screenplay of *A Medal for Benny*.

————. "The Screenplay as Literature," *Twenty Best Film Plays*. New York: Crown, 1943. Contains Nunnally Johnson's screenplay of *The Grapes of Wrath*.

Gussow, Mel. *Don't Say Yes Until I Finish Talking: A Biography of Darryl F. Zanuck*. Garden City, New York: Doubleday, 1971. Discusses the Twentieth Century-Fox production of *The Grapes of Wrath*.

Hobson, Laura Z. "Trade Winds," *The Saturday Review*, 35 (March 1, 1952), 6. Discusses controversial reactions to *Viva Zapata!*

Kazan, Elia. "Letters to the Editor," *The Saturday Review*, 35 (April 5, 1952), 22; (May 24, 1952), 25, 28. The director's reply to criticisms of *Viva Zapata!*

Kline, Herbert. "'The Forgotten Village,' An Account of Film Making in Mexico," *Theatre Arts*, 25 (May 1941), 336–43.

————. "On John Steinbeck," *Steinbeck Quarterly*, 4 (Summer 1971),

80–88. Recollections of filming *The Forgotten Village*, by the director.

Lisca, Peter. "John Steinbeck: A Literary Biography," *Steinbeck and His Critics*, E. W. Tedlock, Jr., and C. V. Wicker, eds. Albuquerque: University of New Mexico Press, 1957.

Metzger, Charles R. "The Film Version of Steinbeck's '*The Pearl*,'" *Steinbeck Quarterly*, 4 (Summer 1971), 88–92.

Pinchon, Edgcumb. *Zapata the Unconquerable*. New York: Doubleday, Doran, 1941.

Steinbeck, John. *The Forgotten Village*. New York: The Viking Press, 1941.

———. *The Grapes of Wrath*. New York: The Viking Press, 1939.

———. *In Dubious Battle*. New York: The Viking Press, Compass Books, 1963.

———. *Sea of Cortez: A Leisurely Journal of Travel and Research* (in collaboration with Edward F. Ricketts). New York: The Viking Press, 1941.

———. *The Moon Is Down*. New York: The Viking Press, 1942.

———. *A Russian Journal*. New York: The Viking Press, 1948.

———. *Their Blood Is Strong*. San Francisco: Simon J. Lubin Society of California, Inc., 1938.

Truffaut François. *Hitchcock*, with the collaboration of Helen G. Scott. New York: Simon and Schuster, 1967.

Tuttleton, James W. "Steinbeck in Russia: The Rhetoric of Praise and Blame," *Modern Fiction Studies*, 11 (Spring 1965), 80.

Womack, John Jr. *Zapata and the Mexican Revolution*. New York: Alfred A. Knopf, 1969.

REVIEWS OF *Viva Zapata!*:

The Christian Century, 69 (April 23, 1952), 510.

Hartung, Philip T. *Commonweal*, 55 (February 29, 1952), 517.

Holiday, 11 (May 1952), 105.

Life, 32 (February 25, 1952), 61.

McCarten, John. "Wool from the West," *The New Yorker*, 27 (February 16, 1952), 106.

McDonald, Gerold D. *Library Journal*, 77 (February 15, 1952), 311.

The New Republic, 126 (February 25, 1952), 21.

Newsweek, 34 (February 4, 1952), 78.